D1160865

Acknowledgements

Many thanks go to all my family members that supported my dream. Also to Steve Skaggs, Kandice Cook, and especially my encouraging husband, Sam for his tireless input and support.

Enormous thanks go to Helen Hart, Director of Silverwood Books in UK and her team. Helen's professionalism and guidance were of the highest of standards in assisting me with editing, and suggestions. Service provided was extremely friendly, timely, and of highest quality. Thanks Helen!

And most of all for the Grace of God in Jesus who worked out my life for his Glory!

Romans 8:28 And we know that all things work together for good to them that love God, to them who are the called according to his purpose.

Unheard Cries

By Joyce Mitchell

Chapter One

Troup County – Autumn 1936

It was picture day at Rosemont Elementary, which meant the entire seventh grade was dressed in their Sunday best. Emma Scott had a perfect part in her shiny black hair, right smack-dab in the middle, with a bobby pin on each side of her head. Today she wore a brand new pair of khaki pants and a crisp white blouse. With her dark hair and tan skin she looked every bit like her Cherokee ancestors; she'd even inherited her mother's sweet smile.

Spitballs were flying from all sides of the one room schoolhouse. In the center of the room stood the old potbellied stove, which was red-hot on one side. The splintered floor around the stove was covered with flaked-off rust-like pencil shavings.

"Emma! Hey, Emma!"

Cautiously (because her mama had threatened to whip her if she got her new clothes dirty) Emma poked her head up to see her classmate Odessa leaning over the top of her beat-up Jean-Prouve desk. Her face was creased with a snub-nosed grin.

"Aaron is trying to get your attention," Odessa whispered, brushing a spitball off her neck.

Emma heard a rustle of paper. Ducking her head, she turned around to see her friend Helen snap her books shut and lean in to whisper a message.

"He said, 'Let's go out back while Mr. Rogers is on break and roll up some rabbit tobacco.'"

Emma looked at Helen in disbelief. "Are you crazy?" she asked her friend.

Helen shrugged. "Not me," she said. "Blame Aaron. He's the one wants to go!"

Through the window they could see the door to the outhouse was still shut tight. But there was no telling how long Mr. Rogers would be in there. Emma had gotten in trouble with Mr. Rogers many times before because of Aaron. He was just so mischievous - and irresistible. Still, Mr. Rogers had an aura of power about him that frightened her. She had the feeling that she was spelling her own doom by succumbing to Aaron, as she knew she would.

Aaron Lerner, the most popular boy in the school, always got his way, not just with Emma, but with all the boys and girls. Being from a wealthy family, he was spoiled. His father and mother were successful farmers and owned the well-known Rock Store on the corner of Hamilton and Salem, across from Pleasant Grove Methodist Church. Aaron's father, Harvey - tall and slender and nearly bald - had been in and out of the hospital recovering from a heart attack that struck him at an early age. Aaron's mother, Bessie, ran the old store.

"Just hold on," Emma said, and tossed her long black hair over her shoulders. She already knew she would go with Aaron, but she wanted to check things out in the classroom before she gave her answer. Around her half the class was occupied shooting spitballs, while the other half had their heads bowed working on their multiplication tables.

Emma leaned way over in her desk; on the top surface, encircled with hearts, was scratched 'A & E'. Her forefinger touched the sticky gum underneath the desk. The niggling sensation of guilt began to fade. She said to Helen in a soft but firm voice: "Tell Aaron okay, but we have to hurry!"

To tell the truth, Emma was feeling a little squeamish in her stomach. But she and Aaron had been out several times before. It was like a ritual for them: they'd sit next to the old well and roll cigarettes; sometimes Mr. Rogers would catch them, sometimes he wouldn't, but when he did Emma would always promise she wouldn't do it again. Usually she meant it too, especially when Mr. Rogers threatened to talk to her parents.

So Aaron and Emma, hands over their mouths and snickering, tried to quickly and quietly exit the double doors. Emma's friend Helen and another kid called Henry, who they all called Runt, followed them just as they had many times before.

In their hurry they nearly knocked the veneer off the wall. Every rusty hinge began to make a shrill noise - to Emma the squeaks sounded like a ship's whistle.

"Good gosh!" Emma exclaimed. "That door is loud enough for the whole town to hear! I just hope Mr. Rogers is situated in that outhouse for awhile."

Henry and Helen, still following Aaron and Emma, burst into laughter. They laughed at anything Emma said - she wasn't the class clown, but she had a great sense of humor and liked to cut up.

"I don't know what he's been eating lately, but he sure has been out of the room a lot," said Emma.

"Probably some of that old corn his Daddy feeds the pigs." Henry said. Everyone chuckled.

"Oh, man - have you ever tasted pig slop before?" Aaron asked. "Every time my granddaddy mixes some with corn meal, my cousin sticks her finger in the bucket to taste it before he pours it in the trough. He told her that she was going to grow long hair on her arms if she keeps eating it."

Aaron grinned. Even when he wasn't smiling, it looked like he was. Emma thought his sky-blue eyes were just beautiful. He was truly the handsomest boy in school, the way part of his black hair spiked up and a spit curl hanged down on the right side of his bangs.

"C'mon," Aaron said, as they ran around the well behind some bushes. "Ahh..and get off my arm!" Henry had been leaning on Aaron all day. Even in the picture that morning he had pulled and tugged on him. Henry was a very bright student, somewhat small in stature, which is how he earned his nickname. He always wanted to be on Aaron's team because he didn't want Aaron to beat him up the way he did some of their other classmates.

It was a little cool outside, still drizzling. Fall was here; dog days had been followed by much harsher weather. Aaron pushed aside the low-hanging dead limbs from the line of brush marking the start of Mr. Perdue's property. One after the other, the four rebels sneaked out of view from the schoolhouse.

Mr. T. Perdue, who owned the property next to the school, was a character. He had a long gray beard and rarely came into town, but when he did he always wore the same dirty blue coverall. His land was just as untidy as he was, with horseshoes, chicken wire, and farming implements strewn everywhere, even overflowing onto the school's property.

"Man, I can't wait to smoke this stuff!" Henry cried.

"Shhhh!" Aaron whispered. He reached way down underneath his sock into his shiny pair of brown and white high-top oxfords and extracted the white rollup leaves he sneaked from the Rock Store basement earlier that morning.

When he thought no one was awake, he had climbed down the basement ladder of his parents' store, pulled out a loose rock from the floor, and retrieved the leaves from an old Prince Albert can. But before he could go back up the ladder, he heard his mother starting up her usual morning routine; stoking the old wood stove so that she could brew some

Louisiana coffee. Aaron waited a long time in the basement - but finally the aroma of that coffee was just too much. He loved strong coffee with fresh cow's milk and two spoonfuls of granulated sugar. He turned around to go back up the ladder and tripped over an old metal box that contained his special marbles, and, of course, every one rolled out.

"Just hope old man Rogers don't smell it on us when we get back in the room," said Aaron.

"Me too!" said Henry.

Aaron and Henry fell simultaneously to the ground and started crawling on hands and knees through bramble to the secret clearing only they knew about. All the while their thoughts were on that old corn pipe and those cigarette leaves - they just couldn't wait to get the good old rabbit tobacco smoke in their lungs.

"Open that box up and get the matches, Henry," Aaron hissed.

Anxiety was setting in—it just took a few seconds to pack that pipe and roll the cigarettes. Henry reached for a long-stem match and struck it on the side of a domino box. The rabbit tobacco plants Aaron and Henry had pulled and dried a few weeks ago were now a beautiful golden brown color, ready to be stripped and smoked. Emma was the first one to get her cigarette rolled. She wanted to smoke that thing and get back into class before Mr. Rogers did. Henry lit her cigarette and leaned over to light Aaron's pipe. They both inhaled at the same time and blew the smoke out their noses. Helen and Henry joined in. After two or three quick draws, they dowsed and pocketed what was left of their cigarettes and scurried out of the thicket back to the old schoolroom.

As soon as all four were back in their seats, Mr. Rogers walked in. He had a very sour look on his face. Emma thought he looked like he had been eating persimmons. Poor man! Couldn't stay out of the outhouse. He was obviously having a bad day.

Mr. Rogers looked around the room suspiciously. Uh-oh, Emma had seen that look before.

"What's going on here?" Mr. Rogers looked at

Emma and then at Aaron; then he scanned the room suspiciously. He sniffed and a look of distaste clouded his face. "Who in this classroom has been smoking?"

There was no answer from anyone, just complete silence. Knowing that Aaron would not break, Mr. Rogers kept his stare dead on Emma. She had always been the one to tell the teacher the truth, even if Aaron gave her a frog on her arm after school each time they got into trouble. Helen and Henry sat very still in their desks, pretending to do their multiplication tables.

Emma raised her hand. "Mr. Rogers, you were gone so long, and I needed a break, so I went outside and rolled just one cigarette."

Mr. Rogers, his arms crossed and his head down, replied, "I know you didn't go outside by yourself, Ms. Scott. Who went with you?"

"It was just me, Mr. Rogers. Really!"

Mr. Rogers looked tired. Beads of sweat dotted his forehead. He knew the day was wasting and he didn't want to spend any more time on this ordeal.

"Well, Ms. Scott, you know I told you that if you broke the school rules one more time I would have to report this to your parents."

Emma hung her head. What a mess. She sure hated to face her mother and dad. At least, she thought, there was the chance her Daddy would be completely drunk on homemade moonshine. "Yes, sir," she said.

She picked up her pencil and tried to focus on her arithmetic. Why had she gone out? Why had she listened to Aaron and the others? Would she ever learn?

Everyone else seemed to be at ease, nonchalantly going through the rest of the day. Finally, while the class was working on spelling, the old cowbell rang. In unison the students put down their pencils, put away their papers and leapt out of their seats.

Mr. Rogers had a piece of paper in his hands that Emma did not want to see. He stopped by her desk.

"Young lady, give this to Con and Beulah tonight."

Emma was staring at her shoes; she took the note

reluctantly.

Mr. Rogers let out a tired sigh. "I just don't know when you are going to learn, Emma! You have to be able to say no to your classmates. I know you didn't think of sneaking out to smoke all by yourself." He watched her, but she didn't move, just stood there hanging her head and staring at her shoes. "You need to learn to be a leader, Emma, not a follower. Do you understand me?"

Emma nodded, desperate to go. At last Mr.Rogers nodded and said, "Go on. Go home. And mind you give that note to Con and Beulah!"

Aaron was waiting for Emma when she emerged from the schoolhouse, leaning casually against a wall with his arms folded and his spit curl flopping over one eyebrow. "Hey, Emma," he said. "If your mom goes to the wholesale house, get her to stop by the store."

Usually Emma's mom tried to go to the wholesale house early in the mornings; salted fish, hoop cheese, and sardines were just about every customer's favorite —not to mention RC Colas and Moon Pies.

"I'll try," she said, still thinking about confronting her parents. She didn't want to be talking to Aaron right now. She really liked him, but she didn't like getting into trouble. He was a little too pushy and was known to act out with that 'Lerner temper'.

The little one-room schoolhouse had emptied out and most of the boys and girls were filing onto the nearly new Blue Bird school bus. Normally Emma rode the bus too, but on this particular day her mother was picking her up so that she could help with the errands. Emma's mother was waiting for her outside the schoolhouse. She slid into the passenger seat and glanced over at the bus.

Aaron had his window halfway down. He was shooting spitballs at the boys walking past, but paused momentarily to wave at Emma. She gave him a half-wave and a smile then settled into her seat for the drive home.

Chapter Two

On the bus Aaron was acting out more than usual. Mr. Thompson, the bus driver, an elderly man who loved children, was usually very kind and gentle; but today he'd gotten more than he'd bargained for. A couple miles down Hamilton Road and his smile had worn off. He'd been watching Aaron in the mirror at the front of the bus and had seen him hit the little boy he'd been bullying ever since they climbed onto the bus.

"All right, young man, that's enough," he said sharply. "I want you to sit down in your seat like the others, and be quiet."

"I'm not doing nuttin' old man," Aaron said, as he turned round and elbowed the boy seated in front of him.

Giggles were heard from the girls and some smaller boys from the back of the bus. A few of them cast admiring glances at Aaron and he smirked, lounging back against the bus window, his long legs stretched over the seat and hanging into the aisle. He sat there listening to the sound of the wind whistling through the crack in the window.

As they passed Pleasant Grove Methodist Church, Mr. Thompson and the kids heard what sounded like the most beautiful harmony in the world. The congregation was singing, "I've Got a Mansion Just Over the Hilltop."

"That's my mama's song, Mr. T," Aaron called out. "She sings in the church choir, you know." He wasn't chatting to be friendly, but to let Mr. Thompson know that he wasn't going to shut up.

"Yep, the Methodists are having an early service today, son," said Mr. Thompson.

The school bus pulled up to the Rock Store near the hundred-year-old oak tree.

As Aaron clambered off the bus, Mr. Thompson hollered after him: "Be careful, young'un! And tell Harvey and Bessie I said hello."

"I will," said Aaron.

Mr. Thompson shook his head sympathetically. "Tell them I really feel for 'em," he said, but Aaron was too far away to hear.

Still a little woozy from the herbal smoke, Aaron knew he had a busy evening ahead of him. He had to pick up the marbles from this morning, help in the hog slaughterhouse, and do any other chores his parents had in mind - although, to be truthful, Aaron's older brother, Thomas, carried most of the workload. Thomas was a hard worker and very active in school. He was one of the better basketball players at Rosemont. He had his eyes on a popular, pretty brunette, Veronica Patrick. Being popular themselves, both Lerner boys always seemed to go for the most popular girls at Rosemont.

The bell that signaled the arrival of a new customer jingled when Aaron opened the door to the Rock Store. The familiar smells of tobacco, animal feed and licorice greeted him when he walked in the door. Reaching for the Lance jar that sat on the counter next to the cash register, he pulled up the red metal lid and grabbed a big Moon Pie; then he walked to the icebox and fished out an RC Cola.

"Hey, Mama," he called out to his mother, who was in the stock room. He didn't wait for a reply but lowered the ladder to pick up the marbles. The old floor creaked with each step he took.

"Aaron, your Daddy had another attack on his heart today," Bessie called down to him. "Dr. Turner made a house visit, said he would be on a lot more medicines, so you and Thomas will have to help ole John clean up - they salted and hung two more hogs today."

"Okay, Mama. Let me get my marbles, and I'll be on my way."

Walking along the side of the store, Aaron could see the guys from the rock quarry digging for mica in their back yard – this was their second week in that spot. He crossed a creek branch and weaved around many cow pies and hay bales before reaching his home, a big white house with the lightning rods and a rooster weather vane on the roof. Aaron went past the front porch to the side entrance and walked in.

Sally, the maid, was cooking tripe – sure did smell good. Aaron reached down into a gallon jug for a couple pickled pigs feet before going in to say hello to his daddy.

Harvey was lying on a cot in the living room, dressed in a white nightgown and nightcap.

"Alright, Daddy?" Aaron asked and Harvey gave him a weak wave.

Dropping his jacket and homework on the hall table, Aaron went on to his room to change clothes for his chores.

"Get that hog in that pen!" Aaron heard someone say through the open window.

John and Pete were out in the field herding pigs and cattle into holding pens. Aaron had put out salt blocks and sorghum grain before he left for school. The words of his mother rand in his head whenever he performed this particular chore: "Aaron, all grazing animals need salt. You've got to give it to 'em so we'll have healthy animals." He also remembered her speech about how valuable their stock was and that someday, because of them, he and his brother would be taken care of financially.

That was just the kind of phooey he couldn't give a hoot about; he wanted his money and fun now.

Just as he was getting ready to work, Aaron noticed that there were a lot of cars and trucks heading south toward LaGrange. Sticking his head out the window, he hollered down to John.

"What's going on?" he asked.

John looked up from his work and at the boy in the window; then he turned his gaze to the traffic on Salem Road. Looking up to Aaron he gave a shrug and went back to his work.

Just then someone hollered at them from one of the cars: "The old courthouse's on fire!"

"On fire?" Aaron was out the door and running through the pasture, jumping piles of cow manure and hay bales, nearly as soon as the words were out of the driver's mouth. He had to go to tell his mother; he knew that some of his relatives had been involved in the building of the courthouse, not to mention it was an exciting event for a town this size. When he arrived he saw a bunch of loggers sitting around on stools, taking their evening break. Some of them choked on their RC and Nehi when they saw the look on the boy's face. Something was up!

"My land, Aaron – what's the matter with you?" Bessie asked.

Aaron tried to catch his breath. "The Troup County Courthouse is on fire!"

All the chatter of the weather and health problems stopped. Everyone was in amazement.

"I can't believe it," said Bessie. She scurried around the counter to get the money from the register. "Closing early," she called out to the loggers. "I'm goin' to see the fire."

Before she closed the drawer Aaron snagged a few dollars and stashed them in his front pocket.

The loggers loaded up in their pulpwood trucks and headed south toward Oak Grove, leaving a trail of smoke behind them. Bessie scattered the burning logs in the wood heater and then hustled out to the porch where Aaron waited. After locking the store door, she grabbed Aaron and the two marched back down the path to the house to see if Harvey felt like riding with them into town.

"This is a big thing – history is being made," she said. "We don't want to miss it."

Bessie helped Harvey put on a new dress shirt while Aaron fetched his Daddy 's jacket and shoes. "Hurry, Mama and Daddy," he said urgently. "We gotta get going!"

"Hold up, son. Take it easy. Don't act like we're going to a fire or something." Bessie and Harvey chuckled together, but Aaron's mouth twisted in an ugly way. He didn't like people laughing at his expense.

"We need to hurry," he insisted. "Don't wanna miss it! Fire could be out by the time we get there."

The three of them hurried down to the car. Harvey needed a little help to get in because he was breathless, but at last they were on their way. Aaron fidgeted and peered out of the windows, straining to get a first glimpse of the fire.

The old courthouse was still in flames when they arrived. It had been drizzling most of the day, but thunder and lightning were not in the forecast. Many businessmen and farmers had gathered on the streets, and fire trucks and emergency vehicles were lined up everywhere. Solid red and navy blue umbrellas, all covered with soot tags, decorated the streets.

As soon as Bessie parked the car, Aaron leapt out, excitement coursing through his limbs. He saw Mr. Duffey, who owned a large packing firm on Hamilton Road. He had made many trips with his parents to Mr. Duffey's wholesale house. "Hey, Mr. Duffey" he called out. "Anyone know what happened here?"

"No, son, we're all in the dark," Mr Duffey said, slicking his greased hair back off his face with one hand. He shook his head, shoulders drooping. "It's a bad business, alright."

Just as Aaron was talking to Mr. Duffey, trying to take in all he could about the fire, he heard a voice coming from across the street. "Aaron, come to the car. Your Daddy is hurting; we've got to get him home."

He looked over his shoulder with eyes of blue fire. "I'm coming," he said. " Just give me a second." He stayed where he was, watching the blazes dance in the clouds. A thick blanket of smoke covered the sky. A second and third call came from across the street. His frozen body finally melted and he jumped the curve, weaved in and out of the umbrellas to find his mom and dad.

"See you later, Mr. Duffey," he called out.

"All right son, you be careful now." Mr. Duffey took a few steps down the street to dodge the cinders.

By the time Aaron reached his parent's car, his head was spinning. His eyes were burning from the smoke, but he didn't care. He couldn't remember the last time anything this exciting had happened in

Rosemont. He remembered his granddaddy 's stories helping to build the courthouse, how long it had taken and what a source of pride it was for the community.

"Daddy, don't you think granddad would be very sad if he were alive, knowing that the courthouse was just about gone?"

"Yeah, I do, Aaron," Harvey said, taking labored breaths in between each word. "He put a lot of sweat into that building, and so did a lot of other good men in Troup County." As he finished speaking, Harvey put his hand over his chest and groaned. His eyes searched for Bessie, who was watching him with a look of grim concern on her face.

"We need to get home now," she said and put the car in drive.

Local citizens began to gather round the blazing courthouse to form a bucket brigade. Aaron and his family drove by the burning courthouse, passing just as two volunteer firemen emerged from the flaming doorway with stacks of singed courthouse records.

Aaron would always remember the day the courthouse caught fire. He often thought of it as the time he truly grew up.

A few weeks later, they heard that war had been declared in Europe, and childhood seemed far, far behind.

Chapter Three

Autumn 1940

Knock knock. The tap at the door roused Emma. She groaned and tried to sit up. She had been very tired lately and had hoped to sleep in. Her nerves had been playing up on her the past few months. She'd finally given in and taken a lot of Goody powders as soon as Aaron dropped her off from the dance last night. Beulah had threatened to call the doctor out. Con just threatened to call Aaron's parents, the real cause for Emma's jitteriness.

As her high school years passed, Emma had continued to date Aaron—at first because she was thrilled by him, but later because he was just always there. And because he was always there anyway, it seemed simpler to say no to the other boys, and carry on dating Aaron.

The tap at the door came again. Wearily, Emma propped herself on her elbow and snapped on the bedside light; at the same time her brother Erbin's dark head poked inside her door.

"Asleep?" he asked.

"I was," Emma said crossly.

"What's the matter with you? Can I come in?"

"You're in - what's in your hand?" Emma asked.

"Your boyfriend, Bully D came by and told me to be sure you got this," Erbin stuck the flyer in Emma's face and grinned. "You know he can't read, but his daddy picked up a stack of invitations at the town meeting and asked him to drop them off in several places. He thought of you first, sis; he wants to take you to a dance."

Both Emma's brothers, Erbin and Orvis, loved to tease her about her friend Bully D, who they referred to as 'Big Ears'. It was well known in Oak Grove that Bully D had been in love with Emma since the first grade. They found this all the more amusing since Emma was the prettiest girl at Rosemont High while Bully D's most notable attributes were his Dumbo ears.

"I'm not going to any dance with Bully D," she said, snatching the poster from Erbin.

"Why not?" Erbin said. "It'd be better than going with mean old Aaron. If you was out on a date with Bully D, why I might even come out with you!"

Con and Beulah had often insisted that Emma's brothers, Erbin and Orvis, go with them on dates, but they'd recently stopped because of Aaron's devilment —Erbin said Aaron was "the meanest person in the whole wide world."

Emma made a face and pushed Erbin out of her room. He complained, but she shut the door hard behind him. Only when she was alone, did she read the invitation.

"Howdy, Friends and neighbors both near and far away,

The Hillbilly Barn Dance will drive your cares away.

We always wear a great big smile and never shed a tear,

We try to spread some sunshine with songs you like to hear.

So, won't you come and join us and spend a little while?

We'll try to make you happy in good old country style,

So, come on to the Oak Grove Hoedown here in Dixie,

For you're always WELCOME to the Hillbilly Barn Dance Party."

Emma let the flyer fall to the floor. Stepping over it without a glance, she opened her bedroom door and ran down the hallway. She screeched open the screen door and then let it slam behind her. She walked down the wooden steps holding onto the handrails, listening to the familiar echo of her steps on the wood. The scene that greeted her outside was one of familiarity and peace. The sound of the blackbirds singing in the tree overhead comforted her. The air smelled warm and inviting, like the invitation from Bully D…

Standing outside with the wind blowing up the amber leaves around her moccasins, she felt like she'd broken out of prison after a life sentence. Last night at the dance she'd told Aaron she didn't want to date him any more. He'd punched a guy for dancing with her, and she'd had enough. "That's it, Aaron," she'd said.

"We're through." Aaron had just laughed, thinking she didn't mean it. But she showed him. She was over him. She was!

And now, with her newfound freedom, there was only one place she wanted to go. As crazy as it was, that place was the Hillbilly Barn Dance Party. For the first time in a long while, she felt like she'd done something right; she felt good about herself.

She jumped up from her favorite spot and went in to deliver the news. Erbin was slouched in a ladder back chair at the kitchen table, a half-eaten biscuit in his hand; he started snickering as soon as Emma walked in. She didn't care. She was going to that dance with Bully D and she didn't care what anybody else thought. She was through with Aaron and his acting out. As boyhood left him, so had some of his charm. Sure, she still liked him… still found him thrilling to be with… but sometimes she didn't want thrilling. She wanted calm, and peacefulness, and safety. Bully D was safe. Aaron wasn't. He had a temper, and that temper had started to make Emma afraid...

Emma pushed her thoughts away and walked down the hallway to the water basin. There she scrubbed her face with her homemade goat's milk soap and dried her face with a starched hand towel. Looking into the mirror she saw a refreshed and smiling face. There was nothing she could do with her crimped hair, but she would worry about that later. The main thing that she was doing something good for herself and she refused to let her fear of Aaron get in the way of that.

Chapter Four

It was a school day. The breeze whistled through the leaves around the Scott house. The sun was shining down and there was hardly a cloud in the sky. The gentle undulations of the old water wheel, turning and turning, accepting the water and then giving it away, was soon interrupted by the roar of a bus traveling up the hill at about 30 to 35 mph. It rounded a curve past the old water wheel. It then raced up another hill before coming to a stop in front of the store where Emma and her brothers were waiting. All three had smiles on their faces and were anticipating the upcoming weekend.

"Mama," Emma shouted as she stepped on the bus. "Don't forget to pick me up today."

"Oh, don't worry, honey, I'll be there at two sharp!" her mother answered.

Beulah had promised Emma a trip into town to buy a new dress for the barn dance that afternoon. It was a bit of a splurge but she and Con didn't care – they would buy their daughter the whole dress shop if she promised to stop dating Aaron for good.

"I worry about her," Beulah had confided to Con on countless occasions. "That Lerner boy is out of control. He's no good for Emma. I think she's beginning to see it… did you know she's told him she doesn't want to date him any more?"

Con always sighed, shook his head, and reached for the liquor bottle again. "Let's just hope it lasts, Beulah. Let's just hope it lasts."

The brothers went all the way to the back of the bus where the bus driver wouldn't notice. Emma found a seat in the middle of the bus next to one of her classmates. As soon as she flopped her bag on the seat in front of her, she leaned over and whispered in her friend's Helen's ear. Helen's mouth dropped and her eyes enlarged.

"You never did!" Helen said. "I can't believe it!"

Emma threw her hands up in the air. "I know, I

can't believe it, either," she said.

Everyone on the bus turned around, legs crossed in the aisles, arms leaning on their knees, to hear Emma tell of her great plans. All of her classmates listened when Emma spoke; she had a friendly nature that people gravitated to.

It had been a real busy day at the store. Beulah had gotten up with the sound of a sick rooster crowing in the wind. She'd prepared biscuits and red-eye gravy for her family. But it was a different story for Con. Beulah had not seen his feet on the ground since yesterday evening's hog feeding. She maneuvered through the door of the corn shed, her stocky body pushing it hard against the shaky lean-to. She pushed a bale of hay back against the wall, lifting a secret door in the floor. His stash was gone. Now she knew why he hadn't been to the store helping with all their regular customers.

Beulah slammed the door on the floor knocking off its rusted hinge. Her face was red, and her blood pressure about to blow its valve. Her heart felt as if it might gallop right out of her chest. This Cherokee was about to take action. She walked back around the store. More customers had pulled in. One was helping himself at the gas tank, the others were in line at the register.

"Ms. Beulah, yo' face sho' is red. What you been doing out there?" a customer and a regular at the store asked.

The skin on Beulah's face was as wrinkled as her unmade bed sheets; her lips were puckered irritably like a fish. She was in the mood to rant this morning and Ole John had just given her an open invitation.

"Ole John, I'm mad at the world today. I've got a busy day ahead and Con is still in bed passed out from his poison moonshine. I've got the store to run and then I've got to pick up Emma from school to get a dress for the barn dance."

"Oh, Ms. Beulah, you oughta get a broomstick and beat the devil outta that man. Make him get out here and help you."

"I know, Ole John. I think I might just do that when I get a break from the store," She handed him a brown sack with sardines and crackers and change from a two-dollar bill. She was tempted to give him the two-dollar bill back; she didn't want any more bad luck, a superstition passed down from her grandmother.

"And you say Ms. Emma is going to the Oak Grove barn dance on Sat'dy? Who she going with, not that mean ole' Lerner boy?

"Thankfully, no. She's going with Bully D, the boy down the road here." Beulah said, and wiped a trickle of sweat from underneath her arm. Circles had formed on both sides of her tattered, out-of-style calico dress.

Ole John started to laugh uncontrollably. "You mean that big-eared boy. Oh, my goodness, Ms. Beulah. Ms. Emma's too pretty to go with that ugly thing."

"Ole John, Con and I don't care who she goes with, just so long as it's not Aaron Lerner. Our girl has been through so much. She doesn't sleep well. She looks like a starveling. Complete bedlam. I, for one, am delighted she accepted Bully D's invite."

The customer behind Ole John had been standing by patiently, but at that he leaned around Ole John's shoulder and expressed to him and Beulah that he had sick children at home and needed to tend to them.

"I'm sorry, sir," as Ole John stepped to the side of the counter to let him get tended to. Beulah dropped his cans of soup and crackers in a large paper bag and lifted it to him over the counter with a smile.

"Ms. Beulah, I know that Lerner boy stays in trouble all the time. I stop by Rock Store once in awhile, and I hear that boy cursing his mother and daddy. I want to backhand him myself sometimes." Ole John waved his hand through the air as if he were swatting flies. "He's just not like his brother. They've never had a lick of trouble out of Thomas. Reckon what happened to Aaron?"

"I don't know, Ole John, he's just mean as the devil himself. All I know is that I'm tired of his mistreating my girl."

"Well, Ms. Beulah, I gotta run. Tell Ms. Emma I hope she has a good time, even if it is with that ugly old Bully D. That is one ugg-ly human being." Ole John turned round to go, shaking his head and laughing all the way to his truck. "Yep, that one sho' is ugly."

It was no time before Ole John had pulled off that Beulah was locking the store to go check on Con. She wanted to give him a piece of her mind, what was left. She followed the path, with the family dog sniffing at her heels. As she got closer to the house she saw an old straw broom on the porch, leaning against the wall. This was a special broom frapped by Emma. It was an extra one from her moneymaking projects at the store. That's one reason she was gonna get to shop big today. Well, one reason.

Leaves and debris were all around the broom showing it had not been put to use lately. It reminded Beulah of what her customer had told her - so she reached down and grabbed the broom, and with force opened and shut the screen door. Down the hall, the door to their bedroom was closed so the children didn't see their daddy in his state. Now she pushed it open and the smell of alcohol and dog nearly knocked her down flat. Seeing Con lying half naked and drooling on their bed only made her madder. Grabbing him by the hair of his head, she pulled him out of bed, threw him to the floor and began beating the fire out of him. Feathers from the stained mattress were flying everywhere. All he could do was mumble. He had not sobered up enough to know what was going on.

"What's wrong, Beulah? Why you hitting me," he asked with slurred speech. Con tried to look over his shoulder at her through matted eyes, but he had no strength at all. Buttons from his smelly shirt were flying through the air with every stroke of Beulah's broom.

"You know what's wrong, Con. I'm sick of your drunk, stinking self not turning a hand to help me. It's been busy out there, and you knew before you drunk all that liquor what we had to do. I'm going into town in a little while and you got to help out at the store."

"I'm gonna' help you. I always do, sweetheart," he said.

"Don't sweet talk me. Just get your self up, shave that gruffy beard and clean up a little bit."

Con crawled up pulling on the leg post with caution. He stood up swaying back and forth, nearly falling back on the floor. He leaned over, pants hanging without a belt and grabbed Beulah's arm trying to kiss her on the cheek. She swatted at him again with the broom. Beulah, cheeks still red, turned around and marched out. She knew if she stayed in that spot any longer it might really get ugly. As she strode across the field back to the store Barky followed at a trot, trying to lick her dusty and bloodstained heels.

Con tried to smooth his thin hair with his hands; there was just a smidgen of blood on his scalp, but not enough to worry about. He went to the table and gulped down a cup of coffee. He wanted a biscuit and piece of streak-o-lean, but he knew he didn't have much time. He didn't want that big Cherokee woman back on him.

He slipped on the tan pants he'd worn yesterday, but he had to find another shirt. This stinky one was missing three buttons. He reached way back in the Victorian chest of drawers and pulled out a fresh ivory colored dress shirt. Slipping it onto his half-cleaned, spindly body, he peered into the mirror. Not too bad, considering. But Beulah would want him to shave. As he did, he ran his hands down his legs to feel the bruising. Wow, Beulah sure gave him a whooping.

The long, slow walk down the path to the store gave him time to feel what hidden damage Beulah had wrought on him. His legs were trembling and he thought they would never get him there. The monkey's noisy chatter sent a sharp pain through his throbbing skull. He slapped the cage as he passed and the monkeys frantically tried to get out of the cage. He walked into the store, but tension was still in the room. He walked over to Beulah.

"How do I look?"

Beulah rolled her eyes impatiently. "Con, I don't have time for your foolishness. Here, take this moneybag and hide it somewhere. I'm only keeping fifteen dollars in the register."

Con walked to the end of the counter, placed the moneybag next to his gun and leather holster underneath a stack of magazines.

"Con, are you crazy? That'd be the first place a thief would look if there wasn't money in the register," Beulah exclaimed. "Take it and put it underneath that stack of logs next to the heater."

"Well, ain't that a crazy place to put it? What if it gets thrown in the heater by mistake?" Then he thought about it and decided it wasn't worth making her mad again, so he did as she told him.

Having briefed Con on what was expected of him at the store, Beulah felt a little better about leaving him. Just in time too, as it was already a quarter til two. Running out the door, she hopped into the old Ford truck and pulled out onto Salem Road in a hurry. The family dog chased her car all the way to the steel bridge. Without giving an arm signal she pulled over onto the curb, got out, and picking up the first rock she could find, threw it at the dog. The dog tucked tail and ran. Finally, she could be on her way. Taking a deep breath, Beulah felt suddenly lighter, free. From here on out it was going to be a good day.

Emma was waiting outside Rosemont High, a big smile on her face. She'd been watching all the boys and girls get on the bus. Aaron turned around as he was stepping up to get on his bus and waved at Emma. To Beulah's annoyance, Emma waved back.

"Does Aaron know you're going to the dance on Saturday?" Beulah asked in a loud voice.

"No, and I didn't mention it at all today," Emma said. "To him or anyone, except this morning on the bus to Helen. But she's a good friend - she won't tell anyone. I overheard some of the girls talking about the dance at school, but I don't think Aaron heard them." Emma got in the car beside her mother. "Oh, Mama," she said. "I can't wait to get to town and pick out my dress!"

"Well then, let's go," Beulah said, and started the car.

Emma settled into her corner, watching Beulah drive. At last she said, "Mama, why is your face so red? And your dress - it's all stained up and all." She reached out a finger to rub a red spot on her mama's shoulder. "There's a little speck of blood right here," she said.

"Oh, that's from your daddy. It's been a rough day, honey. I had the hardest time getting him sober enough to help me. You know what shape he gets in when he drinks that stuff. I had to get the broom after him."

"You must've been really upset," Emma said, eyeing her mama's stained dress.

"I didn't realize I was hitting him that hard," Beulah said. She gripped the steering wheel tighter.

"That oughta teach him," said Emma.

"No, honey, that wasn't right what I did. I was in a moment of anger, but I'll never do it again. That's what I've been trying to tell you about Aaron. He just can't seem to control himself. He has a bad temper. I don't like him hitting you, and I'm not going to have it, and I'm not going to start practicing violence, either. I just want to make that clear to you."

Beulah was talking a lot but she wanted to make sure Emma understood. It wasn't okay to hit.

"I know, Mama." Emma cut in, patting her mother's hand. "I sure wish Daddy would stop drinking. I don't like him that way either."

Emma wanted to change the subject now. Catching sight of the newspaper at her feet, she reached down to pick it up. More turmoil. The front page was all about the drought and all the suffering it was causing, especially in the Midwest. In the headlines, MAN KILLED STEALING TURNIPS!

Seeing her daughter's distraught face, Beulah reached over her school bag and patted Emma's knee: "There's chaos everywhere, honey."

"We didn't lose too much from the drought, did we?"

"Not like a lot of people did. The stream below the house helped us a lot. It never got dry. We got to water the garden, the grass, the animals and the flowers from that stream. But don't you remember, a bunch of our vegetables kept disappearing though."

"I do remember. We never knew what happened to

our squash and green beans. You know, Daddy kept telling both of us that someone was stealing the veggies, but we thought he was making all that up."

Emma gave her mother a warm smile.

Some of the pink was disappearing from Beulah's face now, but the stains on the shoulder and under the arms were still there. There appeared before them a sign saying Main Street, next right. They were there. Thank you, Lord.

A large line of people was waiting outside the Employment Office. People were hustling to and fro, trying to get in line. On the other side of the road was a row of parlor games and cafes. People were lined up at the movie house, trying to forget their everyday troubles for just a few hours. Past the theatre were a large line of sharecroppers and farmers, applying for aid on their parched farmlands. All this was depressing to Emma - the war, the economy - but nothing was going to hinder her shopping for that special barn dance dress.

Town was crowded today. The news of the hillbilly

hoedown brought many customers in. Beulah stopped in front of a store with a red awning that said Mansour's Department Store.

"Let's park here and cover both Solomon's and Mansours."

"Okay," said Emma. She glanced over her shoulder in one of the windows. A man's white dinner jacket was on one of the mannequins. Next to it was a beautiful apple-blossom pink gown, fluffed sleeves and a sweetheart neckline. She stood there daydreaming for a minute, imagining herself in that gown, its petticoats swirling around her knees as she danced.

Meanwhile, Beulah put a penny in one of the newly installed parking meters and started talking to one of her regular customers.

Something caught Emma's eye and she walked a few feet away. She peered into the window of a little corner café. Inside she could see a nice couple seated at a table for two, having a steaming mug of tea. The lady, shoulder length curls, was dressed in a beautiful burgundy-colored dress with shoulder pads. The gentleman had mutton chop sideburns and a gray suit with a burgundy-gray striped tie. At one point the man reached across the table to hold the lady's hand; the couple looked deeply into one another's eyes. The man looked sharp in his nice suit, just how she imagined Aaron would look one day. Sure, she wasn't dating him at the moment, but she still liked him… and a girl could dream.

Emma could picture herself sitting comfortably at that little wooden table across from Aaron, sipping a chocolate milkshake through their sweetheart straws, and looking deeply into one another's eyes. She looked down at the sidewalk. Her hair fell back down to her shoulders. She could feel her cheeks warming behind the curtain of hair and she was glad her mother couldn't read her mind; she'd give her a long lecture if she so much as mentioned Aaron's name.

"Emma," her mother said eventually. "Quit daydreaming. We need to find you a dress for the dance. Your father will be expecting us home early. And in any case I don't trust him at the store, not when

I know he's got a second stash of moonshine tucked away somewhere."

"Yes ma'am," Emma said.

"C'mon young lady, which shop do you want to browse in?"

"Let's try here," she said, pushing open the door to Mansours Department Store.

A nice saleslady with a pageboy bob approached them. She was wearing a sweater and perfectly tailored mid-calf length skirt, and looked every bit like one of the models in the department store catalogue.

"May I help you?" she asked.

"My daughter is looking for an evening gown to wear to..."

"Let me guess," said the saleslady. "The Hillbilly Hoedown."

"How'd you know?" asked Emma.

"Have you noticed outside? The streets have been

congested all day. Our store has sold eight dresses so far, and expect to sell many, many more," said the saleslady.

Just then the doorbell jingled, announcing the arrival of a fancy redheaded woman with quick, eager eyes. The saleslady left Emma and her mother immediately to go attend on the rich lady. Emma watched, her jaw hanging open in amazement, as the lady tried on a fedora, took one glance in a mirror and snatched it off her head. With a flick of her dainty wrist, she threw it down on the counter.

"How about that one," Emma heard her mother say. She turned to see her gesturing toward the showcase window. There was the lovely pink dress that caught her eye as she entered the store. It was beautiful, but seeing it on the pale-skinned mannequin, Emma could tell it wasn't the one for her.

"It's okay," she said.

Leaving her mother to inspect the stacks of purses, hose, scarves and hats that lay amid the colorful dresses, Emma wandered over to a rack on the far side of the store.

Something caught her eye. There, hanging over a display of high-heeled shoes, was a beautiful royal blue dress, exactly the same cut as the one in the window. Goose bumps rose up along Emma's arm. "Oh, Mama," she breathed. "Would you just look at this?"

Beulah came over. She reached out and gently stroked the fabric of the full skirts. "Emma Scott," she said softly. "You have exquisite taste. This dress could have been made for you and your coloring."

Emma unhooked the dress from the rail, laid it carefully over her arm, and went straight to the dressing room. She slid the dress over her head, zipped it up, took one look and knew that it was the one. She slipped on the matching gloves, with sparkling sequins, turned around once to look in the mirror. That was all it took. She looked exactly like a princess.

"That was quick," said Beulah.

"This is the one, Mama," Emma said. "No doubt about it. Can I have it? Oh please say yes…"

Beulah smiled as she pressed a ten into her daughter's hand.

Emma paid for her items at the cash register, got her one-fifty in change, and walked out. Her eyes were ablaze with brown fire.

"Now, I can't wait until Saturday night," she said linking arms with her mother.

She skipped and danced all the way down the street, even bumping into a little girl who was busy reading Dick and Jane and not watching out where she was going. Alarmed, the little girl ran to catch up with her mother.

"Hey, Mama. I'm a little hungry. Can we get a bite to eat?" asked Emma.

"Well, young lady, I guess so, since you only took a few minutes in the store," said Beulah. "And I want to tell you, you looked so pretty in that dress. You're going to be the prettiest princess there... I mean the only princess there."

"Thank you, Mama."

They drove through the crowded streets and headed to Nash's Barbecue place to get a barbecue and a pint of chocolate milk, Emma's favorite. Con would be happy, too, that they didn't spend all day in town, and that they'd thought of him when ordering barbecues. Emma even thought of her two brothers, who would be helping her daddy after they get off the bus. But most of all she thought about the Hillbilly Hoedown, and her new dress, and the way the petticoats would feel as she danced. Oh, she couldn't wait!

Chapter Five

Saturday evening came at last. Erbin and Orvis plowed a path to the well, drawing buckets and buckets of water, getting ready for Saturday bath time. After all, this was a big day for them, and for Emma. They could wash that weekly filth off, feel fresh and their big sister had accepted Bully D's invite to the Hillbilly Barn Dance at Oak Grove Community. Maybe, just maybe, they'd get to tag along in hopes of snagging a girl for themselves.

Red roses were blooming in Emma's bedroom, fresh and unfaded. They'd come from Bully D. As soon as he'd heard the news that Emma would be his date, he placed the order, wanting the prettiest the florist had for this special person. He was a wonderful boy, a hard worker, but just a little on the ugly side. Emma had to listen to her brothers all day, snickering about Bully D's elephant ears each time they passed by her window going to the well.

Emma had been feeling a little squeamish all day, lightheaded, and wondered if she had made the right decision. Aaron had not been pleased when he heard she wasn't going to the dance with him. He'd scowled and for a moment she'd thought he was going act out. She'd stared him down, her heart beating fit to burst, and eventually he'd turned on his heel and walked away.

Simply thinking about how she'd felt when he scowled made her cry. She pulled a handkerchief out of her sleeve and mopped at her tears. Just then, her mother walked by her door, turned and came in to sit on the bed. She placed her hand in Emma's, and put the flat of the other hand on her forehead to see if she was feverish. "Are you all right, Emma? You've been acting a little strange today. How do you feel?"

"Oh, I feel fine, Mama," Emma said with a sniff. "I have to admit I'm afraid Aaron will show up at the Barn dance tonight."

"Oh, perk up. I don't think Aaron would dare show up. And if he does, don't you worry - your brothers are going to be there, and Bully D is fine strapping boy who can protect you." Beulah stroked her daughter's hair. "Don't cry any more, honey. You're young— you don't need to be tied down to one boy, especially one like Aaron. Now cheer up. You and Bully D are gonna have a wonderful time."

She reached in her checked apron and pulled out a box. "I want you to wear these earrings tonight." This was just one of the keepsakes Emma's grandmother had passed on down, not counting the big inheritance, enough for Con and Beulah to build the grocery store.

"Are you sure?" asked Emma. Her tears dried and her eyes lit up with brown fire, just like the sparkles on the diamond earrings.

"Yes, you're going to be the prettiest girl tonight." Beulah slid off the bed, stood to her feet, reached over to give Emma a hug.

She gave her mama a tight hug in return, with the sweetest smile ever.

"Now that's the spirit, Emma."

Her mother went out of the bedroom and made her way to the kitchen. Con was chucking the woodstove, and flakes of rust and ashes covered the wood floor. He was hungry, patiently waiting for Beulah to console their daughter, waiting for those brown biscuits and fried salmon patties. And a pickled pig foot, too.

Emma wanted so much to feel good. She had scenes flash through her mind all day of the times she'd gone on dates and Aaron showed up and showed out, whippin' her date. He has freedom to date whomever he chooses, she thought, but he doesn't give me the same. She tried to empty her head of all these painful thoughts, but they kept coming back. She had not only prayed for good weather tonight, but that everything would go smooth.

It was six o'clock. Emma glanced in the mirror. Her swollen, tear-stained face was looking much better. Time to get ready.

She reached for the royal blue gown and matching gloves. It took only a few minutes to put her hair in a French twist and powder her nose; she was born with dark, curly eyelashes and didn't need to use black Mabelline. She reached down on her cluttered vanity for candy-apple red lipstick, leaning into the mirror making sure she was picture-perfect. Just in time.

She heard Bully's loud muffler on his truck way down the road. He rumbled his way into the driveway next to the store. He stepped out, walking past the deep-red amaryllis in bloom. Emma could hear her brothers' laughter. Oh my lands, she thought, this is embarrassing - sure hope Bully D doesn't hear Erbin and Orvis.

Bully D walked up on the porch, kicking the black and white yard dog as it nibbled at the hem of his new khaki pants, stumbling to reach the yellow stained door that Emma was already hanging out of; she was ready to go before he saw her two brothers. Bully D's big red ears were shining; he had a sparkle in his eyes. Emma placed her hand on his arm and smiled up at him.

The beauty and the beast were ready for the hoedown.

Bully D drove fast to the Oak Grove Community

where the big barn dance was already in motion. Several deer crossed out in front of them. Before he and Emma could find a parking place, some roosters crossed over too.

"Sure are a lot of animals out tonight. Must be having a party of their own," chuckled Bully D.

"Look, look at that little fawn," she said suddenly, pointing out of the car window. "Look at its long slender legs. I bet the mama is around here somewhere."

"Yep, sure would like to have my rifle with me right now," said Bully D, as he searched for a parking space.

"You wouldn't shoot that little thing, would you?" asked Emma.

"Betcha boots I would," he said.

"Are you a hunter?" she asked, interested.

"Sure am - me and my daddy both, we love to hunt. We go all the time. We hunt for squirrels and rabbits mostly. And Daddy likes to catch em'catfish out of the lake. Sho' is good eating," he said. A smile lit up his face and made him seem a little less ugly for a moment.

Emma sat there so content - something she never felt with Aaron. Maybe Bully D couldn't read or write, but she was enjoying every word he said. Looks are not everything, she thought. With good-looking Aaron, she was always sitting on pins and needles not knowing what to expect.

Cars and trucks were lined up and down the road. Colorful signs and balloons decorated the highway, pointing the way to the Hillbilly Barn Dance. Probably everyone in the whole county had seen those signs, there were so many strewn about. If you traveled north, south, east or west, more than likely, you would've seen posters advertising the big barn dance.

Emma sorta got quiet in Bully D's truck. Anyway, the sound of his truck was so loud she had to holler when she did speak. "I sure hope Aaron won't show up tonight," she said in a shaky voice, the truck not missing any bumps.

"Well, if your brothers get to come, and if he does show up and starts a fight, we three will just have to beat the fire out of him."

Emma laughed. But deep down in her heart, she knew that Aaron was strong and probably could whip all three. She'd seen him put both her brothers on the ground.

Bully D turned the truck and did another pass-by, still looking for a parking space.

"Why don't you pull around the barn close to the big oak tree, Bully?" Emma asked.

"That'll be a lot of walking for you," he said. "You don't want to snag that pretty blue dress you got on. What's the matter? Are you afraid Aaron will be here or someone might see you riding with me?" He grinned. Bully D knew he was one ugly man. He did have a mirror at home. But he had such a good sense of humor he'd tease with other people about his own ugliness.

“No, it’s not that,” she said.

Aaron being at the dance probably would bother her a bit more than someone seeing her with an illiterate and “not so cute” guy. “Oh, well, just pull in where you want to,” she said.

Bully D parked pretty close to the oak tree, but not as far as Emma intended him to. After all, she had conceded to go with him to the big barn dance, and he sure didn’t want to get her mad now. He stepped out, went around and opened her door. He took her hand so she wouldn’t fall out. She reached for her clutch bag and slid down to the foot rail on the old logging truck. On the way down something on the seat snagged her dress and she felt a moment’s panic. She put her hand behind her to pull the dress up, checking it for a tear. Please, she thought, don’t let it be damaged. Not this lovely dress. She felt a wave of relief when she saw that it was fine. No damage.

Bully D closed the truck door and held out his arm for her. She hesitated a moment, then placed her hand on his sleeve. A feeling of guilt swept through her and she tried to push it down.

"Are you okay?" asked Bully D.

Emma hesitated. A voice inside her head was telling her not to date other people. But she knew this was not a date. Or was it? Another voice told her not to feel guilty. She thought back to the tenth grade. She remembered her teacher, Mrs. Cottle saying, "Emma, you don't have to be afraid of Aaron. He runs over you because you *allow* him to." All manner of thoughts were running through her head. She tried to stop trembling, but now she just couldn't.

"Emma, it'll be alright. Come on girl, let's go dancing," said Bully D. His voice was so tender. He had concern and affection.

Bluegrass music was blaring through the loft as they entered into the barn. People scattered around on the dance floor turned toward them and stared. Some pointed. Some put their hands over their mouth and giggled. Bully D didn't care; he'd brought the prettiest girl in the county, maybe the state, to the Hillbilly Barn Dance.

Bully D and Emma, both red-faced, walked over and spoke to some of Emma's girl friends at Rosemont. Most of them looked kindly at Emma and Bully D, especially Emma's friend Helen, but one of the girls bent over laughing until tears began to run down her cheek.

Bully D shrugged. He really didn't care that they were poking fun at him. Emma minded a little, but she came to have fun and wasn't going to let their teasing her spoil it. "Come on, Bully D," she said. "Let's dance."

Bully D needed no second asking. He pulled Emma to the center of the floor and started doing the jitterbug—he could really cut a rug.

A couple of hours later Emma, face still red hot, left Bully D at the edge of the dance floor and went to get a cup of cold ice water. She was really having a ball. Just then her brothers walked in. They had walked part of the way and hitchhiked the other. Emma was glad to see them, but only if they weren't going to tease her; she'd heard enough about Bully D's ears for one day.

For Orvis and Erbin it couldn't have been further from their minds; they'd seen too many pretty and good-smelling girls on the floor to be thinking about their sister. Neither brother was bashful. The two handsome guys stood in awe at all the girls in their crinolines and lace.

Emma was having the time of her life. She was going to dance with Bully D some more when she felt someone tag her shoulder. But this tag was a bit harder than the others.

Emma turned around, her heart pounding. She'd almost guessed who it was going to be, and she was right. It was Aaron.

"Aaron, I didn't know you were here," Emma said in a nervous tone.

"I heard you was gonna be here," he said, "so when my chores were done I thought I'd come down and take a look." He looked her up and down. "You're lookin' mighty fine, Emma."

"Thank you." Emma spoke softly hoping she

wouldn't make Aaron mad. But he already had a strange look about him. "Mama took me to town this week and bought me this new dress just for the dance."

"Can you spare me a dance?" Aaron asked. His hands were already reaching for her waist and she knew she couldn't say 'no'.

Slow music was playing, and Aaron pulled her in close and she caught a whiff of the alcohol on his breath.

"How'd you get here?" he said as they moved to the center of the room.

Around them, the other dancers swayed, the girls' dresses a kaleidoscope of colors, but Emma barely noticed them. All her attention was on Aaron. "Bully D invited me the first of the week," she said. "I rode with him in his logging truck."

Abruptly and without a word, Aaron broke loose from the slow dance. He left Emma standing there and ran around inside the barn looking for Bully D. He couldn't find him, but he heard his voice just outside.

Bully D had bought an RC Cola and had his feet propped up on an old beer keg in the straw. He had been having so much fun, but was completely exhausted.

Then suddenly—Wham! His legs were knocked off the keg and his whole body hit the hay pile.

"Man, I'm telling you, don't you ever dance or speak to my girl again," Aaron said in a fiery voice. He hit Bully D as hard as he could with his fist. This stunned Bully D and he staggered to his feet and fell back down, this time striking his head on a rusty John Deere cultivator.

The music stopped. Everyone's eyes widened with disbelief. Emma ran over, but Aaron pushed her aside. She felt a strange shiver running down her back as she looked into Aaron's intense eyes. "Are you crazy?" she said. "Why did you hit him? He didn't do a thing."

"It's your fault. You shouldn't've been here on a date with Bully D or anyone else," said Aaron, scathing as he pressed his hand hard on her shoulder.

Emma felt the old fear come rushing back. "It's not my fault," she said. "It's not anybody's fault but yours." She was tense with anger - every muscle in her body wanted to hit Aaron, but she knew better.

Several people had come outside and were towering over Bully D. The barn host called out for someone to call an ambulance. Bully D had a deep gash just above his left temple; he'd lost a lot of blood.

Tension was still on the dance floor, like a coiled snake, waiting for the slightest disturbance to make it strike. The disturbance came when the barn door opened. It was Orvis and Erbin.

They'd heard from some hillbillies their big sister was in trouble. They ran toward Aaron, but he was a quick thinker, and he held out both arms and ran right over the both of them. Then he snatched Emma by the arm, dragged her past the onlookers and shoved her into his mother's borrowed car.

Emma struggled, protesting. "Let me go!" she said. "I want to see if Bully D is okay."

"He's okay," Aaron said through gritted teeth. "It's just a bit of blood."

"A bit of blood?" Emma glared at him. "There shouldn't have been any blood! You shouldn't've knocked him down, Aaron. He didn't do anything wrong."

"He did," Aaron snarled. "He took my girl on a date."

They were in the car now, driving fast, all the way down to the river. Aaron slowed the car to a halt and jumped out.

Emma went barrelling out after him, fear and fury raging through her body. "I'm not your girl. I told you, we're not dating any more. I can see who I please."

Aaron's eyes flashed like blue fire and he reached out and caught hold of her arm. "You're my girl," he said again. "Say it. Say that you're my girl."

Emma felt the fear pulsing through her, all the fury gone. Her heart was racing and she felt breathless. She shook her head.

"Say it!" Aaron gave her a shake. Then suddenly, without warning, his arm snapped back.

Emma didn't see the blow coming, but she felt it. His fist came up hard against her face and she felt a rocket of pain. Stars exploded in her mind. She staggered back, but Aaron caught her and held her to him.

"I'm sorry, baby," he muttered. "But you make me so mad."

"I-i-i-it's okay," Emma stammered.

But it wasn't okay. Her eye swelled and went black, and she had to put makeup over it before she went to school the next week. And meanwhile, Bully D was taken to the city-county hospital. He had a concussion. A warrant was served for Aaron. He was taken in, but his mother and Daddy got him out the same day. Bully D got out of the hospital the following week, but it took longer for Emma's black eye to heal.

Chapter Six

Con stepped in. It was time to put all this turmoil on the back burner.

He called Emma to the breakfast table. "Emma, your mama and I have had a long talk about this rebel boyfriend of yours. We're sick and tired of seeing him abuse you. We're gonna put a stop to it, one way or another. When I go into town, I plan to stop by the Rock Store and try to talk some sense into that boy."

"Oh, Daddy. You can't!" Emma twisted her hands in her lap. "Why don't you leave it alone? I can handle Aaron."

Con stared at his daughter, taking in the black eye and the downcast face. "But honey," he said gently. "It don't look to me like you can handle him. Your mama and your brothers and me – we're sick of seeing you upset and coming home with bruises. It's time I stepped in."

Emma knew there was no point in arguing. She popped up out of her chair, ran to her bedroom, and threw herself on her bed. Sobbing, she buried her face in her feathered pillow. She loved Aaron and did so much want him to change, but she was scared for herself and for her dad, and the idea of his talking to Aaron frightened her. What if Aaron was drunk? Even worse, what if Con was drunk?

Con got up and made his way out of the house, head down and hands in his pockets. Beulah stood at the window watching him go. She had never seen Con this upset. Maybe his visit to the Rock Store could put a stop to some of this chaos. Actually, she couldn't believe that he was sober enough to do anything.

Con was making a trip to the wholesale house to restock his store. He pulled out on the Salem Road toward town, looked to his left at some black clouds rolling in. It was a gloomy day. But Con was on a mission. He pulled into the Rock Store yard. It was a little crowded around the store so he pulled past the old big oak tree. At once, a gypsy lady came running up to him trying to make a sale. He shook his head that he wasn't interested, walked up to the chimp showcase, which was a place to show various pets to draw customers into the store, and picked up a peanut that someone had dropped and fed it to the little monkey. He walked into the store. Some of his regular customers were there and spoke to him by nodding and waving with their sack in hand as they went to get in their vehicles.

Con lucked out. There in the store was Aaron and his parents. They were all gathered around the cash register. He asked Harvey if he could talk to them.

"Of course. What's on your mind?"

Con began to tell Emma's story of what happened at the hoedown, how Aaron had kidnapped her from the dance floor and drove down to the river and beat her because she rode to the dance with Bully D.

Harvey and Bessie both turned to look at their son. Bessie pulled Aaron aside. "Aaron, you didn't do it, did you? Tell me you didn't beat up Emma."

He laughed out loud. "Mama, you know that old man is lying. People are always lying on me. You gotta believe me."

"Really?" asked Bessie, her eyes searching his face.

Aaron looked affronted. "Who you gonna believe, Mama – that old drunk, or me?"

Bessie nodded and turned to Con with disgust. "Aaron says it's all a lie, and I believe him. Now get outta –"

Con broke in, cutting her off. "Bessie, you got the most rotten child in the county. Everybody knows it. And someday you're gonna be sorry!"

"Get outta here, Con Scott, you old drunk," Bessie said.

"I ain't going until this rotten kid promises to stay away from Emma." Con stood straight and faced Aaron, putting his right hand in his front pocket and touching the small cold pistol. "I'm telling you, Aaron, stay away from my house and my daughter."

Aaron waved his fist in Con's face. "You can't keep me from seeing Emma," he sneered.

"I can," he said. "You'll see." He twisted on his heel and went straight for the door. He could feel their eyes burning into his back.

It was a long ride back home. It was all he could do to keep from turning around and going back to the Rock Store to whip that little rebel.

When Con reached his house, Beulah was waiting for him, a stricken expression on her face.

"What is it?" he asked.

"It's Erbin," she said quietly. "He's gone and joined up." "Joined up?" The words didn't seem to make sense to Con. "What do you mean – joined up."

"I mean he's gone and joined the U. S. Army."

Con stared at her. Whatever next? War in the home— and the world at war!

He reached for an opened gallon of homemade whiskey and turned it up.

Beulah stared at him. "Is that all you're going to do?" she asked. "Get drunk?"

Con took a swig and then followed her as she made her way into the store.

Con and Beulah worked silently for a while, serving customers and stocking shelves. Before long, Con heard a truck pull up outside, and then the sound of running feet. It was Aaron. He came into the store looking for all the world like a bull about to charge.

"You dare come on my property and threaten me, old man?" he said, feet planted wide and hands on his hips, chin thrust forward aggressively. "No one does that. No one intrudes into my home and talks to me or my family like that!"

Con said nothing, and that seemed to make Aaron madder. In a sudden fit of vengeful rage he set in, screaming uncontrollably inside Con's store.

Beulah was behind the counter serving up salted fish to a customer. She, like Con, kept a pistol close by. Her big brown eyes watched. She could hardly make out what Aaron was saying; it was so loud and echoes were bouncing off the wall.

Then the barely audible sound of a siren in the distance was heard. The siren grew louder and louder. Aaron had been incarcerated so many times that when he heard how close the sound was he hit the counter with a thundering crash. Pieces of glass stabbed into his bare arms. He directed one of the most evil looks toward Con before running to his father's truck and heading the opposite way of the incoming vehicle. Any time he would hear the sound of a siren he would flee the opposite direction. Aaron stayed away for a while. He started writing letters to Emma, trying to sweet talk his way back into her life. "I promise you, Emma. I'll get some help. I'm going to church now." He promised her that he would change. He was on the front pew every time the church doors were opened at Pleasant Grove Methodist, sitting right next to his mother singing about heaven.

Emma watched him from the other side of the church. Part of her yearned for him, he was still her playmate from school, her favorite date, the guy she most wanted to be with. But part of her couldn't forget the black eye he'd given her after the hoedown.

The assistant pastor offered free counseling to Aaron and Emma. In secret, she joined him regularly in the small church office. Aaron had not missed an appointment, and on the last day Aaron promised Emma that everything would be fine now.

"Please, please promise me that," she said in a quavering voice.

Aaron stayed silent, but looked contrite and Emma felt a tug at her heart. She loved this boy, no matter what.

Aunt Lolla, the church secretary, saw Aaron and Emma on their last visit. She followed them to the door as they went outside to walk to the Rock Store. Aaron was a couple of steps ahead of Emma when Lolla shouted: "Don't worry! Just be happy."

Aaron pretended he hadn't heard Lolla and kept on walking, but Emma nodded at her. Everything's okay now, she thought.

Chapter Seven

Georgia – 1942

Aaron and Emma were married in West Point, Georgia, in 1942, pledging to stay together till death parted them. Would the marriage really last forever? Emma hoped it would. She could remember clear as day the time Aaron had proposed to her. He'd gone down on one knee, holding her hand, his spit curl over one eye looking for all the world like he had back in school. She was torn… he was the one for her. Wasn't he?

Deep down in her heart, Emma knew. There was just too much unhappiness already. She had to make this marriage work.

Both sets of parents came to the wedding, as did Emma's brothers and Aaron's brother, Thomas, and his wife, Veronica, who was a sweet plump woman with a smile that lit up a room. A nice reception was held at Pleasant Grove Methodist Church with much of the food provided by Aunt Lolla. The tables were draped with white lace and ribbons of many colors and everything was perfect in style for a typical southern wedding.

Something happened at the reception that Emma didn't like to think about later—an indication of how things were going to be.

"Hey brother!" Aaron said with a little grin in his voice. "How are you and sis doing today?" He leaned over and gave Veronica a tight hug—which seemed to go on and on. Veronica wriggled a little, trying to escape. Emma could see she looked none too comfortable.

"We're fine," Thomas said, and slapped Aaron on the shoulder. "Come on, Aaron, let my wife go. You've got your own now." His smile showed he was trying to make a joke, trying to keep Aaron sweet.

Still smiling but obviously irritated, Aaron let Veronica go and abruptly grabbed Thomas in a headlock.

Thomas struggled, going red in the face. "Ouch, that hurts. Turn loose, Aaron."

But Aaron—wiry and strong—just laughed and squeezed harder. "You oughta know better, big brother," he said. "You 'member when us boys would wrassle around the house, I always got the best of you."

"Aaron, let him go," Emma said. "People are looking."

Aaron glanced around the room and saw that all eyes were on him. He let Thomas go suddenly.

Thomas staggered a little, then smoothed his hair with one hand, eyeing his brother warily. "Sure, I remember, whatever you say, little brother," he said.

Veronica sighed. She gave Aaron a sharp nudge and nodded towards the open door. "You'd better go find a seat."

"Yes, ma'am," Aaron said sarcastically. "What'ere you say, sis."

He strode out, Emma hurrying behind him. She glanced apologetically at a few people, caught her mother's eye, and quickly looked away.

Con and Beulah had been against the marriage; they didn't want Emma to marry such a high-strung person. But once the proposal had been made and Emma had accepted, it seemed Aaron and Emma were hell-bent on getting married. So, as a gesture of good will—and because the store and their farming business had flourished—Emma's parents bought them their first single-story bungalow on Salem Road, about two-and-a half miles from their home and about three miles from Rock Store.

"Oh, Daddy!" cried Emma, the day Con gave her the keys to her new home. "It's lovely. I'm going to make Aaron a wonderful home!"

"Well, let's hope he makes you a wonderful husband," muttered Beulah, looking sour.

"He will, Mama," Emma said. "He's changed. You know he has." Without waiting for a reply, she hurried up the pathway to inspect her new property.

The little L-shaped house stood fifty feet from the Salem Road, a persimmon tree hanging over the roof and beautiful flowers in front and on each side of the house. It had a small porch with three steps out front. Behind the house were a stream and lots of trees, and straight out back was a single-seated outhouse. Guineas and peacocks covered the place, and three baby goats kept the grass "eat up" around the house.

The newly-weds moved in, and for a time things went smooth as silk. Aaron was sweet and attentive, and marriage seemed to have mellowed him. When Emma told him shyly that she was expecting a child, he scooped her up in his strong arms and kissed her face all over.

"We're gonna be the best mama and papa that this town ever saw," he swore.

In October of the next year a beautiful baby girl was born. Aaron and Emma named her Judy Ann. She had pretty blue eyes from her Irish side and jet-black hair from her Cherokee side. Her cousin, Timmy, the son of Thomas and Veronica, was born in May of the same year.

Uncle Willie, who had built Aaron and Emma's house, also built one for Thomas across from Rock Store. Veronica and Emma's children played around Rock Store while the girls helped Bessie in the store. Harvey, too, was very active in the business when his heart wasn't acting up. Months went by and the store's profits were better than ever.

And yet, events soon proved that family life had not done anything to dampen Aaron's fiery streak.

On one cold winter day a gas truck rolled up to the store, and a man got out to fill the tanks. Judy, who was still too young to understand what she was saying, said some bad words to him. Veronica overheard her, and was quick to give Aaron a piece of her mind.

"Aaron, don't teach Judy and Timmy those words. You should be ashamed."

Aaron, with mischief on his face, just laughed. "Shoot, Veronica, I've taught 'em a bunch a words that'd turn your face candy-apple red. I think it's pretty funny."

Later that year Aaron got into a fight with one of his former playmates from Rosemont. They were in the old red barn on Lerner Road, smoking and drinking liquor, and Aaron's anger flashed. The other man's mother called the law, and Aaron was incarcerated once again. He would have had to stay in jail longer—but his mother paid his way out.

"Ms. Bessie," the county deputy said softly to her, "you know you're not doing the right thing by paying him out every time, don't you?"

Bessie replied loudly, "He's my son. That's what a mama does. I love my sons."

"Yes, ma'am, I know you do," said the deputy, "but Aaron's never going to learn his lesson if you keep bailing him out."

Without another word Bessie and Aaron left and got in her shiny black car. The deputy's statement began to gnaw at both of them. When they got to Aaron and Emma's house, Aaron got out, slamming the door hard. He walked in the house swearing and throwing furniture.

Emma was in the bedroom putting Judy Ann to bed. She came running out.

"Aaron – what's wrong?" she cried.

"Nothing's wrong!" he shouted, and kicked a chair so hard it splintered against the opposite wall.

"Aaron, no!" Emma begged. "My Mama gave us that chair…" and she ran to set it upright.

"Leave it," Aaron said. He twisted round, his eyes narrowed as he searched the room. "Why ain't the table laid for supper?"

"It isn't supper time yet," Emma said. "I was putting Judy Ann to bed, and then I thought I'd do some meatloaf."

"Meatloaf? Meatloaf? What kind of meal is that for a man who's been out at work all day, huh?" Aaron made a grab for her arm. "What kind of wife are you, that let's her man starve? There should be food on the table and a drinks in the fridge for me the minute I walk in that door."

His eyes flashed their old blue fire and Emma felt the fear in the pit of her stomach. He hasn't worked a full day in his life, she thought. He was the same old Aaron that he'd always been. "I'm sorry," she said, knowing it was best to agree and not get him madder. "Let me make your supper now."

"Now isn't fast enough," snarled Aaron. He jerked her arm and she tripped, falling sideways into him. That made him even more angry, and in a flash his fist had come up. Emma hardly saw the blow coming. She had just enough time to shut her eyes when the world exploded in pain.

The blows came fast then. She held her arms up in front of her face to protect herself, backing away towards the door. Aaron followed her, shouting incoherently, his fists pounding against her. She felt her lip split and tasted the saltiness of blood in her mouth. Then she was at the door and from behind her came a tiny voice. "Mama?"

It was Judy Ann. She'd heard the noise and got out of bed, her ragdoll trailing from one hand. She stared up at her mother and let out of a howl of anguish. The sound seemed to make Aaron into a wild animal. He swore and cursed, and grabbed Emma by the hair.

"Go to bed, sweetie," said Emma, urgently.

But it was too late. Aaron had reached down and grabbed Judy Ann with his free hand. "Shut up that noise!" he yelled.

But Judy Ann cried louder, her wails rising to an ear-splitting scream as Aaron let go of Emma and slapped the child. Emma screamed. Judy Ann sobbed. Aaron slapped her again, until at last Emma caught his arm and begged him to stop. "She's just a child," she said. "Let me put her to bed. You sit out on the porch, Aaron and rest from your hard day at work. I'll drive out and get us some barbecue..."

But it was too late. Aaron was gone. He'd turned on his heel and stalked out of the house. She heard the sound of his truck as he took to the road at high speed.

Emma scooped up Judy Ann and hugged her close, crooning to her until the child calmed down and finally went to sleep. She curled in the bed with her daughter and waited for her husband to come home, watching the clock work its way round to 1am… 2am… 3am…

She didn't see him until morning, when he came back hungover and white-faced.

Chapter Eight

1946

It was a beautiful day. The sun shone down from a clear, blue sky. Birds chirping in their nest sent a glorious sound through the air. A sweet smell of honeysuckle was coming through Emma's window, but she didn't feel quite right. Her stomach looked like a balloon fixing to pop. She'd been miserable carrying this baby. She came close to many miscarriages, but it wouldn't be long before their second child would be born.

Emma was lying on the sofa, being melancholy. Aaron had left last night at dinnertime and had not been home all night. After the kinfolk had brought in food and placed it on the table, he snatched up a fried drumstick and disappeared. He was always ready to hit the road without much regard for the rest of the family.

It really irritated Emma to have thoughts of Aaron.

She wished he would act normal like his brother, Thomas, and that he would keep a job. It bothered her that they had to depend on Aaron's parents for everything. Emma felt her nerves stretched beyond endurance.

Judy Ann was just a few feet away outside in the yard. Emma could hear her playing in her sand box with her little bucket and shovel they'd picked up in Florida last year. There were voices coming through the window. Emma waddled across the room to lift the blind to check on Judy Ann. She thought her trembling legs would never get her there. She peeped out. It was Aaron, clothes all slouched - he'd finally returned home. He was throwing a little red ball to Judy and tickling her under her arms until he had her crying.

There was a sound of a car pulling up. Emma pressed her nose to the window to see who it was. Odessa, slender, shiny blond hair and all decked out in plaid, stepped out. Odessa flipped her hair back over one shoulder and slammed the car door. She glanced up at the house for a moment, searching the windows, before picking her way down that path and making for the yard at the side.

She crouched down by Judy Ann. "Hey, sweetie. How are you? Aint you just the image of your mommy now?"

She totally ignored Aaron.

Aaron folded his arms across his chest. "Hey, Odessa. Ain't you gonna speak to me?" he asked.

Odessa ignored him. She played with Judy Ann for a few more minutes. Then she straightened up, brushed down her skirt, and walked across the yard like she owned it.

Emma was waiting for her in the kitchen.

The two women exchanged a quick affectionate hug as best they could, although Emma's belly kept them apart.

"Odessa, it's so good to see you. What are you doing in this neck of the woods?" asked Emma.

"Oh, it's been awhile since I'd seen you. My

husband is on a business trip and I thought I'd swing by and catch up." Odessa perched on a stool at the table and crossed her elegant legs.

All this time Emma was thinking ahead. She'd known Odessa a long time and could tell by her face there was more to this little visit. She was up to something.

Emma reached for two glasses and poured them some lemonade. "I sure miss those good ole days at Rosemont," she said. "We had the most fun, didn't we?"

"Sure did, Emma. I miss it a lot." Odessa tapped a cigarette on the table and lit it. She inhaled, looking at Emma with eyes narrowed. " How's the family? It looks like you're ready for the hospital."

"Oh, I am. I've been having a lot of cramps lately. I just don't feel quite right."

"So... how are things with Aaron?" Odessa asked.

Here we go, thought Emma. This is really what she came for—to talk about Aaron.

"He's doing okay, I guess," Emma said. "He's not here much, to tell the truth."

Odessa straightened in her stool and peered out the window. Emma followed her gaze and saw that he and Judy were sitting on a large rock throwing sticks in the stream.

Odessa put her cigarette to her lips, drew on it, and let the smoke trickle out in stream that curled upwards around her nose. "Well, Emma honey, I heard a rumor and thought you should know."

"What is it?" asked Emma. She felt a sinking in her heart. She had a feeling she knew what was coming.

"I heard from a friend that Aaron was at the dance hall last night," Odessa said. "He was drinking and having a real good time. Apparently he left with Renee Grubek, and you know that she's a piece of trash. She lives down the road from me. She tried to go with my husband…"

Emma had thought her spirits couldn't sink any lower, but as she listened to Odessa, she felt as if the life had drained out of her.

Suddenly Odessa trailed off, and both women became aware that Aaron was standing at the door watching them. Emma pressed her hand to her side. She didn't know how long he'd been there, whether he'd heard everything Odessa had said.

Odessa flushed. She ground her cigarette out in the glass ashtray on the table and hopped down from the stool. "Well, Emma, I gotta go," she said. "Good luck with the baby… and give Judy Ann a kiss from me."

There was a long silence in the kitchen. Emma stared at Aaron without speaking. Eventually she heard Odessa's car speed off.

"What's for dinner?" Aaron asked, smoothing his hair back from his brow casually. How could he be so cool, Emma wondered. An image of him with Renee Grubek flashed through her mind and she thought she would throw up.

"I can't believe it," she blurted out. "When you didn't come home last night, I hoped it was 'cause you had a flat tire, or your Daddy was sick. How could I be so stupid? I should have known you were up to no good." The sentence ended on a scream. "I hate you. I should've listened to my mama and daddy."

She picked up the ashtray that Odessa had used to grind her cigarette out in and slung it toward him. Butts and ash flew out, staining the air. The heavy glass barely missing his head came down with a crash. His hand shot out and he grabbed her round the throat. "What are you saying?" he demanded, teeth clenched tight. "What are you saying, Emma? You saying I was with Renee Grubek last night—is that what your dumb friend told you…?"

"You're hurting me," Emma gasped, clutching at his hands and trying to back away.

Just about that time Judy Ann walked in.

"Let me go," Emma begged.

Aaron threw her down to the floor. Judy Ann screamed.

"It's okay, baby,' Emma said, scooping the child to

her as best she could around the bulk of her belly.

Aaron swore and kicked the stool. It shot across the room and splintered against the wall. He strode to the cupboard, grabbed his moonshine and went out of the house.

Emma held Judy Ann tight and began to weep. A pain swept up through her belly, swiftly followed by another. She bit her lip hard and prayed for it to stop.

That night a second child was born to the Lerner family. Larry Owen, a dark-haired boy with big brown eyes, came into this world. He was already familiar with the violence in this home from being in his mom's tummy for nearly nine months.

Aaron arrived at the hospital after the birth. Emma couldn't bring herself to speak to him. She just lay back against the pillows, feeling exhausted. She watched Aaron through the open doorway as he passed out cigars to everyone in the waiting room.

"What are you going to call your little boy?" one of the old guys asked Aaron.

"Buck," Aaron said. "I think I'll call him 'Buck'."

For Emma, the next few years passed in a blur of babies and nappies and night feeds. She tolerated Aaron at the house, when he was there - which wasn't often. He'd taken to staying out late, drinking and seeing other women. After a while, Emma stopped learning their names. She didn't care any more. If they kept Aaron away from her, then that was fine by her because she was better by herself.

In March 1948 a third child was born into the Lerner family — Betty, who had dark hair like her brother and sister. Aaron and Emma decided to call her by her middle name, Betty Jo. Interestingly, this little girl nearly escaped being in the Lerner family. When it was time to leave City-County Hospital, Emma and Aaron's mother Bessie got in the ambulance with a very cute little baby. When they arrived home, beautiful flowers from several merchants around town were taken out of the car first. Suddenly a cry — not from the baby — came from the ambulance.

"Oh no, Emma." Bessie shrieked. "This is not Betty

Jo. We've brought a boy baby home."

Emma looked down, picked up the little arm, and on the little black-and-white beaded bracelet read a boy's name. "Oh land, I can't believe it."

Aaron gave one of his mischievous grins and said, "Hey, that's okay—I wanted another boy just like Buck anyway!"

Bessie got back in the ambulance, went to the hospital, and explained that they had been given the wrong child.

The nurse on duty said, "Oh, Ms. Bessie, please don't tell my supervisor 'cause she will fire me."

Bessie sighed. "I'm tired, and I'm not interested in telling anybody. I sure don't want to go through any red tape. Just give me Betty Jo, and I'll go home." Bessie certainly was tired—she had a lot of pressure on her these days. Harvey had been ill again in the past few months, and Bessie had to run her own home, the store, and even Emma and Aaron's home.

The elderly nurse breathed a sigh of relief. "Oh

thank you, thank you, Ms. Bessie—God bless you!"

Aaron and Emma's fourth child, Emma Jean, was born prematurely. Still, she was a dark, curly-haired, beautiful baby, with the prettiest blue eyes Emma had ever seen. Like Larry and Betty Jo, she had heard so much turmoil while waiting to be born that she no doubt wished she didn't have to come into this terrible environment.

Aaron was abusive to the whole family. At the beginning of his acting out, several family members and friends got involved to try to put an end to it, but they soon saw that they couldn't fix the problem—they found out the hard way that if you called the law on Aaron, you would pay for it after he was released.

One time when Judy was very young, a drunken Aaron grabbed her and drove her down to a deep spot in the river. As they pulled up, Judy was frightened at the sight of a Georgia bobcat watching them from the bank; but it didn't move when they drove up.

"Sit by that tree," Aaron commanded. "You'll be okay."

Of course, Judy obeyed.

She watched her Daddy put on his waist-high rubber boots. Then he walked into the water and started turning an instrument that looked like part of an old telephone. To Judy's amazement, fish soon began to float on top of the water.

"Daddy, what are you doin'?" she asked.

Aaron laughed. "Fishin'! When I turn this crank, it shocks the fish." After gathering up a bunch of the stunned creatures, he took Judy and the fish home and told Emma to clean them.

One hot summer day all the Lerner children were playing hopscotch, ring-around-the-roses, and London Bridge in the yard under the big oak tree. As usual, they were playing outside so they would disturb Aaron as little as possible. Betty Jo and Emma Jean went down to the spring to get a cold drink of water in a gourd. As they came back toward the house they heard their daddy 's loud voice coming from the little bungalow.

"Betty Jo, Jean—get over here." Aaron said with a

grin, coming out into the dusty yard. "I'm going to draw a circle and put you two in it and see who can whip the other one. And you better fight hard, 'cause the one that loses gets a whipping from me."

"But, Daddy, we don't want to," said Betty Jo.

"I said do it! Aaron hollered. "I'm your father, and you do as I say, you hear me?"

The two little girls hurried into the circle he'd drawn.

Jo was skinny and a couple of inches taller than Jean, but Jean was a little heavier. Today it turned out that Jean won, and Betty Jo got the whipping. There was no question, though, that the fight was exciting to watch. Both girls were mean as rattlesnakes and cursed like sailors. How else could they be? After all, that's all they saw around the house. Their father was a thief, liar, and any other immoral word you could think of. He was the definition of depravity.

Chapter Nine

1954

BANG! POW!

Metal seemed to be flying everywhere. An elderly lady in an old beat-up car had lost control in the curve just out front of Rock Store. She had been speeding and ran right smack into the big oak tree out front, barely missing the showcase chimp cage. Small pieces of shattered glass fell onto the dirt and few green patches of grass around the store. The chimps were going crazy, one climbing the cage and the other dancing in the sparkling glass surrounding its feet, making all kinds of squawking noises. A shiny piece of bent metal lay beneath the cage like someone had been playing horseshoes.

Betty Jo and Jean ran from their play to peek out from behind the corner of the store. Larry had been sneaking moon pies from the Lance container next to the Coca-Cola box, and he'd been popped on the arm and was sent down a ladder to the store basement earlier that morning. Marbles flew from his hand when the accident occurred.

He screamed out, "Mother, Mother, can I come out now?"

Emma looked around, didn't see Aaron close by, and hollered through the store, "Yeah, Larry, come on up, there's been an accident out front."

Larry, wiping away tears from having been in that dungeon, skated across the milky-way marbles and climbed the shaky ladder.

Emma gave Larry a tight hug. She, for one, didn't care how much he sneaked out of the cookie jar, anything to stop the rumbling in his little flat stomach. Emma loved her children. She did her best to protect them. But she was tired, and age was catching up with her.

They all went to take a look at the scene of the accident. Blood was everywhere, in every wrinkle and crack in the old lady's face; it was spattered on her apron, which was covered with flour, grease, and dough. An ambulance arrived a few minutes later and covered her with a white sheet. The children watched in horror. The world seemed to be a brutal place.

Judy hadn't joined them. Earlier that morning she had cut her foot when she was running from the Rock Store to the big white house to get Harvey to come and stop Aaron from hitting Bessie and Emma.

"Grandpa! Grandpa!" she screamed. "Help!"

Aaron had seen her go, and his rage swelled. "Get back here!" he yelled. But the girl didn't stop, so he swiped a shampoo bottle from the shelf and threw it hard. It smashed right in front of her and she was going so fast she couldn't stop. The glass had cut her feet to ribbons. Emma had spent the rest of the morning picking glass out of Judy's feet.

Even though the excitement for one day had been overwhelming already, there was more to come.

"Emma, get the car and drive me to the Barker house," Aaron demanded.

"Oh, here we go again," she muttered under her breath. She pulled the car around, and Betty Jo, Larry, and Jean jumped in. At first Betty Jo got in the back seat with her siblings, but she immediately climbed over in the front seat to sit between her daddy and mama. She noticed an eighteen-inch-long knife lying on the floor near the seat.

Everything went fine for a few minutes. Everyone was talking about the accident they had just witnessed in front of Rock Store.

A new 1954 Chevy passed by as they were going down Fox Hill nearing the Salem Road Bridge over Flat Shoals Creek. Emma caught a glimpse of a familiar face. Was that her mama driving the car? Did they have a new motor?

Wham! Came a slap across Emma's face. She gasped for breath, her eyes smarting. "Aaron, what–?"

"I told you, don't look at your mama and daddy when we meet them. I've told you and told you!" Aaron yelled.

"I didn't mean to look at them, Aaron, I promise." Emma said as she wiped tears with her hand. "I saw a car, but I didn't know it was them, I swear. I haven't seen them in weeks. I didn't know they had a new car. I didn't mean to look at them, honestly."

"Yes you did, you liar." Aaron roared, and slapped his sobbing wife again. In the back, the children started to cry out too. Her knuckles turned white as she gripped the wheel tightly.

The noise of the children in the back seemed to make Aaron even more mad. He cursed and aimed another slap at Emma.

"Daddy, stop!" Betty Jo screamed, compelled to protect her mother. But even as she spoke, she knew the consequences.

Aaron turned on the little girl. "Shut your mouth, Betty Jo. You shouldn't even be up here in the front. You're always stuck up here. Get in the back seat where you belong." He picked the five-year-old girl up and threw her over the seat, right into Larry's face. Larry loudly burst into tears, crying and crying.

"Shut up, Buck. I'm going to stop this car and beat the devil out of you if you don't stop that whining. Little boys don't cry."

Unable to do anything but wait for the storm to pass, Emma looked out the driver's side window. How did I get myself into this mess? Why didn't I listen to my mother and father? They tried to tell me—what am I going to do now? Will we ever be free? One phrase struck her. It seemed to sum everything up: lonely impasse.

They passed over Flat Shoals Creek and went up the hill. The road took them past Emma's parents' store, which was locked up—not surprising, considering the fact that they had just passed the owners.

The kids looked as they passed the store. As usual, Billy and Mike, the family's pet monkeys, were in their cage next to the grocery. Larry had stopped crying by this time and he began to reminisce. "Mama, when can we go see Mama Scott and Daddy Scott? We ain't been in a long time."

"And you probably won't ever see them sorry folks again," Aaron snapped. "I told your mama and y'all not to speak to them. They're good for nothing."

He grabbed the wheel from Emma, nearly causing her to lose control. "Just sit back and keep quiet!"

Emma kept quiet. Her eye was hurting where his ring had caught her in a back-handed slap, and had started to swell. She rued the day she was born.

God, why me? Why me? It was not the first or the last time she would ask that question.

Larry and Betty Jo began to laugh about the time the monkeys were in the store, throwing ketchup and food off the shelves at Daddy Scott. Suddenly they had heard sirens from emergency vehicles going down Salem Road, and the monkeys immediately walked to their cage and closed the door.

"That was so funny," Larry said, stifling a giggle. Betty Jo and Larry would look at each other and laugh as silently as possible—they didn't want the monster to hear them. Meanwhile, Jean was being a sweetie pie, sitting in the middle and playing with her little rag doll.

Finally, they reached the Barker house. Aaron pulled into the moonshiner's yard. Some law officers had just made a purchase and were pulling off. The back yard was full of cars, both new and old, and logging trucks. Betty Jo peeked out the car window and realized it was a yard full of drunks, all of them exchanging money and goods for moonshine. One gray-haired man brought Mr. Barker a salted ham and received a gallon of moonshine in return.

The family waited for several hours while Aaron did business with old man Barker and hung around getting drunk. Eventually they got back in the car, and Emma drove north on Salem Road. As she approached the Burr Arch Truss steel bridge, she could see a luminous sight. It really looked strange. Was it a ghost? She thought it might be—after all, years before someone had tied a rope over the top of the bridge and hanged himself. There were sightings of ghosts in that part of Troup County, just as about as many as in

Heard County where the psychic, Mahaley Lancaster lived.

Aaron was nearly passed out, so it seemed safe for the children to talk. Larry asked his mother, "When we were at Daddy Scott's one day, what was that man doing? You know, that man with the pointed white hat. Remember? You could only see his eyes, until he took his hat off."

Emma remembered. Larry was talking about the day he and Judy and Betty Jo were outside playing with Barky, the family dog, and several Ku Klux Klan vigilantes had approached Con, asking him to join them over in Alabama. Daddy Scott had cursed them and told them to leave, that he wanted no part of their group.

"Oh yeah. I remember Mama telling me about that incident," said Emma. "She said your Granddad ran them off. He pulled his gun out of his holster and waved it at them."

The KKK men had left in their old truck, and Con had never seen or heard from them again. But before they had gone, one of them reached down and picked up an old broom made out of grass that Beulah had frapped together. He lit a match to the straw and threw it in Con's store yard next to the twenty-five-cent-a-gallon gas pump, near the five-cent Coca Cola sign. As soon as the men disappeared, Con and Beulah went outside and stomped it out.

Chapter Ten

Pleasant Grove Methodist Church

Halloween Tacky Party

Saturday, Oct. 31st

Ages 5 - 8

PRIZE FOR MOST TACKY COSTUME

PRIZE FOR MOST BEAUTIFUL COSTUME

Please Come!

Costume Judge, Mrs. Lolla (Church Sec.)

The big Blue Bird bus rolled down Hamilton Road and made a sharp turn past Pleasant Grove Methodist Church to turn into the Rock Store yard. The stop sign on the bus came out, the door opened, and Larry nearly fell out of the bus. He'd seen the Rock Store church sign across the road. He ran inside the store. "Mother! Mother! Can I go to the tacky party Saturday?"

"What party?" Emma asked, as she handed Bully D his change from the cash register.

"The tacky party, at the church. I'm seven, and Betty Jo is five, so she can go, too. It's gonna be so much fun. Please, please!" Larry begged.

Aaron had been lying on the floor next to the stove. He stuck his head up when he heard Larry's voice. "Hey, Buck, you can go. There's a big dance at Tanglewood this weekend. I plan on going, and when the Halloween Party is over, you can ride with your mama to pick me up."

Emma rolled her eyes, then glanced over at Bully D. Bully didn't say a word, but he knew from Emma's look that she heard some upsetting news.

Aaron crawled out of his hole on hands and knees and wobbled over just to put a headlock on Bully. "Hey, Bully D, you wanna go?"

"No," he said, "I've got to work all day Saturday, and I don't dance anyway."

Bully was saying he couldn't dance just to throw

him off, but the truth was that he was a great dancer.

"Aww, you could learn. And there'll be some pretty girls on the floor. You can wear that pretty blue shirt we gave you for your birthday."

Bully D broke away from the tight hold Aaron had on him. "No, thanks not this time. Well, I'd better get home. Mama and Daddy will be looking for me. See ya'll tomorrow." Bully D smiled at Emma on his way out. He let the door slam louder than usual. He wanted to whip Aaron so bad.

Emma helped get Larry and Betty Jo ready for the tacky party. Larry tied a handkerchief around his head, smudged his face, tied a rag to a broomstick and threw it over his back. He went as a hobo.

Betty Jo dressed up like a gypsy. She had on a red skirt with a black blouse and a pair of costume high heels. She tied a tight band around her shiny black hair.

Emma walked the two children across the road and watched as they entered the church. Word had spread. People from all over Troup County had come trying to win the "big" prize. There were firemen, witches, more hobos, clowns, doctors, and girls dressed like movie stars.

Later, after Emma had dropped Aaron off at Tanglewood Dance Hall, she placed Jean on her right hip and went back to the church to see if Larry and Betty Jo were ready. Betty Jo stood there empty-handed, but Larry stood tall with a "big" prize in hand—a great big brown teddy bear. He had won the prize for being really, really tacky. Emma gave both children a hug. "That's good, Larry. Did you win anything, Betty Jo?"

" I came in second," she answered, "but only first place got a prize."

"Hey, that's alright, as long as you had fun."

"We did," said Betty Jo. Both children had smiles on their faces. It had been a fun day and made a change from dodging Aaron's temper.

They went home and ate some dinner, then soon enough it was time for Emma to pick up Aaron at

Tanglewood Dance Hall on Whitesville Road. Betty Jo and Jean crawled into the back seat, yawning and rubbing their eyes because it was so late. Larry and his mother got up front. Judy wasn't with them. Earlier that morning, Aaron's great aunt, Helen, came by the store to see if Judy wanted to go home with her for the weekend. Since Aaron had big plans of his own, he let her go.

Great Aunt Helen, Harvey's sister, was a college graduate. She was tall with dark hair and blue eyes. She always said that Judy favored her in her earlier years, and that Judy was her favorite out of all the Lerner children. She and her husband weren't able to have children and had asked Aaron and Emma many times in Judy's early years to let them adopt her.

Now, Emma drove down a long, narrow dirt road. It wasn't midnight yet, but pitch dark and very spooky. She did not like being out with just the kids. She and the children pulled around the building and next to a chinaberry tree. She pointed her headlights toward the dance hall and told Larry to walk down there and let his daddy know they were there to pick him up.

"It's too dark, Mother," Larry whispered. "Ya'll go with me."

Emma told the kids to get out of the car. She held Jean tightly on her hip and proceeded to the dance hall. Larry and Betty Jo followed.

Emma opened the door and looked all around. It was so dark on the dance floor, but she could see many couples slow dancing.

"There's Daddy," said Jean excitedly.

Emma glanced the way Jean's little finger was pointing. At first Emma thought Aaron was dancing by himself, but as she drew closer to him, she saw he had someone pulled up tight.

"Who is that blonde haired girl he's holding tight?" asked Larry.

"That's his dancing partner," Emma said tightly. "Go tell him we're ready, Bubba." Bubba, Buck. Larry had many nicknames.

"Yes, ma'am."

As soon as Larry approached him, his daddy put his hand on Larry's shoulder and turned him toward Emma.

"Tell your Mama go to the car, I'll be out in a minute."

Larry, ears red and burning, carried the message back to his mother. Aaron and the blond continued their slow dance, her head stretched around Aaron to check out his wife and family.

Emma and the kids sat in the car for hours. Jean and Betty Jo fell asleep in the back, curled up together. Larry and Emma waited and waited. Bright headlamps pointed their way, as each car left. All but two cars had gone. Finally, Aaron took the girl to her car and he was grinning from ear to ear when he got into the family's car.

"Get in the back, Buck," Aaron said with urgency. He climbed over the seat, waking up the girls.

Emma was about to speak, but Aaron silenced her.

"Don't say a word," he hissed, showing her a tight fist. "Just follow behind that car."

He'd adhered to the blond and wanted to go the last mile—her blinkers were on and she made a right turn toward an old farmhouse. Emma breathed a deep sigh of relief. It had been a long, long night. She wanted to get her little ones home to try and get some rest.

Chapter Eleven

"Meow! Meow!" A gold and white cat flew past a customer's head as he entered Rock Store. Aaron was on another rampage. A nice-looking deliveryman had just left the store, and Aaron was accusing Emma of looking at him. He had Emma's arms behind her back like he was trying to tie a knot in them.

Suddenly his rage was gone. "Hey baby, go get the car and the kids—I'm going to fill the tank with gas, get some money from Mama, and we'll go down to St Mary's and Jacksonville. We'll stop by that fishing hole on the way."

Emma was stunned at the sudden turnaround. She never knew what to expect from Aaron. "What? Are you sure?"

"Yeah, we haven't been in a while—it'll be fun."

Emma glanced at Bessie to see if she was going to

say anything, but she didn't. Not a soul, even his own mother, was going to question Aaron when he said to do something. Probably Bessie thought this would be a good break for her and Harvey. After all, Veronica could help in the store.

Emma reached for some sardines, cakes, and crackers, walked to the house, picked up a few items, and cranked up the car to leave. She knew that she and the kids didn't need much—they would have to sit in car most of the time while Aaron frequented the joints.

On the way down Highway 27, as they were nearing the Florida line, Aaron saw a couple of hitchhikers.

"Pull over," he said. Just to make sure Emma was listening, he took a bottle opener and ran it roughly up and down her right arm. Emma pulled over without signaling.

Emma certainly didn't like the looks of the two men. Lord, help us! she thought. Aaron reached down and shoved the knife he always carried under the passenger seat.

Two scruffy men in their mid-thirties got in the back seat of the car.

Aaron turned around and smiled at them—he could always be charming when he wanted to. "Where y'all goin'? Lookin' for work?"

The taller of the two said, "Yeah, we're headed down to Jacksonville to see if there's any construction work."

The other one chimed in, "There wasn't much going on up North. Weather didn't want to cooperate, so we thought we would head south."

The four Lerner children were in the back seat when the new passengers got in, but Judy soon climbed over to get in the middle of the front seat. Jean quickly followed her, clambering into the front seat and sitting in Judy's lap. Betty Jo wasn't scared of the strangers, though. In fact, she wanted to find out more about them. She had never seen these people before, but they seemed friendly. They had gladly accepted some of the whiskey Aaron had turned around to offer them. Soon he was Indian wrestling with each one. Of course,

Aaron won each round.

As soon as they stopped to fish under the bridge at St Mary's, Georgia, the hitchhikers got their belongings and headed on toward Jacksonville.

The fishing didn't last too long—soon, at Aaron's command, Emma was driving to the nearest beer joint in Jacksonville. Whatever her instructions were, that was just what she did.

Hours went by, but Aaron never came out. Finally Emma took a risk and pulled Buck to her side. "Go on in there and tell your daddy let's get a motel."

Buck obeyed, but it did no good. "He acted like he didn't even hear me, Mother."

Emma sighed. It was dark now, and late, so, as they had done many times before, she and the children bedded down in the car.

A couple of days later the family was at a different beer joint somewhere in Florida—Aaron inside, Emma and the kids waiting outside—and Emma bought a newspaper to help pass the time. She gasped when she looked at the front page. There were pictures of the two hitchhikers they had picked up on the way down. They had robbed a store and put the storeowner in the trunk of his own car.

"I wonder if that man was dead that they put in the trunk." Judy said, wide-eyed.

"Probably was," said Larry.

The trip to Florida had really affected Emma's nerves this time. She and the kids were so tired, having been locked up in a car for days, just waiting on Aaron sewing his wild oats. Her bruises were still showing and she was in a lot of pain.

Emma and Judy plotted to get away which would not be the first time. Many times Emma had left because of the fear of Aaron, but her love for him seemed to always lead her to return.

One evening Aaron had bought someone's moonshine that was really potent, and he passed out for a long, long time.

Bully D pulled into the store yard, coming in to buy

his RC Cola and can of sardines, but before the purchase was made, Emma pulled him by his overalls and shoved him to his truck. Judy had gathered Larry, Betty Jo and Jean. They were hiding in the floorboard of the old beat up logging truck.

"We've got to go, Bully D. Hurry before Aaron wakes," Emma said excitedly.

"Where you goin' this time, Emma?"

"Take us to Daddy's store."

"I did that last month, Emma, and you piled yourself back up here. You gotta make up yor' mind, woman. The sheriff has tried to talk to you - yor' mama and daddy has tried. Wake up! You got to get help for yourself and for your kids," Bully D blurted out.

"I know, I know." Emma said, her eyes pleading with Bully D to help them. "I will this time. I mean it."

Bully D pulled in to the store yard on Salem Road. Several cars were waiting in line for the gas pump. He sat there with loud rumblings coming from his stomach. Emma had been in such a hurry; he didn't even have time to gulp a cola down. Bully D dropped his passengers off and told Emma good luck.

Daddy Scott was tending to the store. He looked up and stared at them. "Emma?" he asked. "You coming on a visit? I thought you wasn't supposed to come see us no more?"

"It's more than a visit, Papa," Emma said. "I'm not going back."

Con Scott nodded. "About time," he said. "Go inside and see your mama."

The kids scurried past Billy and Mike's monkey cage. Betty Jo came to a complete stop, turned around and went back to the cage. There was only one monkey. Billy was not in his cage. Where was Billy? She ran behind the others as fast as she could to find Mama Scott to see where Billy was.

Larry was first to reach the porch of the Scott's house. He opened the door and went right to the kitchen. Mama Scott was toiling over the hot wood stove frying streak-o-lean and redeye gravy. Cathead biscuits were pulled from the oven.

All the kids ran and gave Mama Scott a big hug.

"Lands!" she said, wiping her hands on her apron and hugging them back. Her eyes went to Emma and the two women looked at each other over the children's heads. "You visiting?" she asked. "Or staying?"

"We're staying, Mama," Emma said quietly. "If you'll have us."

"If I'll have you…?" Mama Scott gave a sad smile. "You always have a home here, Emma. You know that."

Betty Jo just couldn't wait to ask: "Mama Scott, where is Billy?"

"You're not going to believe this, Betty Jo. Everyone wash up and I'll tell you at supper."

There was a blue and black speckled tin basin sitting in the kitchen, and all the children took turns dipping their hands in the cloudy water. Betty Jo and Jean ran to Mama Scott and swiped their wet hands across her stained apron. Everyone found a place in Mama Scott's kitchen. Betty Jo squirmed fast to get a place by Mama Scott. She wanted to hear loud and clear. She loved Billy and Mike so much, and so did the other children.

Mama Scott looked sad as she told her story. "Yesterday, real early, before the roosters started crowing, we heard these awful sounds coming from behind the house. Your granddad said it sounded like coyotes and bobcats were fighting back there. Last week one of our neighbors said he'd seen a mountain lion deep down into the woods, close to the pond.

"Well, anyway, I went to open up the store and I noticed that the cage was open. Mike was inside, but Billy was missing. So I fed Mike and left the cage door open, thinking he'd return. So before the sun went down, we decided to close the store early and take a walk into the woods to see if he was out there playing somewhere in the trees. We'd gone down about a hundred feet and looked up in a sweet gum tree—there was Billy's skull tightly pressed between two limbs.

Your granddad and I think that a mountain lion attacked him."

"Oh no!" Betty Jo exclaimed. "I'm gonna miss Billy." She and her siblings were almost in tears.

"Well now, you must take care of Mike because he's gonna miss Billy, too," Mama Scott said.

Con Scott came in just then and sat down at the head of the table. He looked around at the big family he suddenly found there. "So, he said at last. "Y'all staying?"

Emma looked at her kids one by one. They looked back at her, their faces eager but unsure. She knew what she had to do. "Yes, we're staying," she said. "This is our home now."

And so they stayed.

Chapter Twelve

When she was six years old, Betty Jo was always disappearing. On one occasion, Mama Scott and Daddy Scott searched the store and the house. Then Mama Scott went to the chicken house, and there she was sitting in the chicken coop with the mama hen and her baby chicks. She was all huddled up, with her knees against her chest, chin cupped in her small hands, and her back against the wall peeking through the octagon-shaped chicken wire. She was afraid that her daddy would creep up behind her. She was in a place that she could see out clearly, but you'd hardly notice her if you glanced in the chicken pen.

She had reached in to get an egg, and a huge chicken snake had entangled itself around the eggs. There was a big lump in the snake's throat from a swallowed egg. Betty Jo also had a lump in her throat; she started screaming to the top of her voice, "Help. Somebody help. Get me outta here."

Mama Scott's patience was wearing thin. She reached for Betty Jo's arm. "Betty Jo - we were worried about you. You gotta quit this hiding. Nobody's going to bother you around here. Now you let somebody know where you're playing, young lady."

"Yes ma'am," was all she'd say.

Another morning before the sun shone bright on Betty Jo's dark head, she sat under an old wicker chair outside next to the gladioli and sunflowers, pulling seed out of each flower. She was very nervous, and would look over her shoulder when she heard any kind of sound. She knew her daddy would be coming to the Scott house; she just didn't know when.

Betty Jo heard a voice a short distance away. It was Mama Scott; she had snatched up a brown and white speckled hen and was wringing its neck. Then she put it on the chopping block, started plucking feathers and burning the hair off. That was just too much for Betty Jo. She ran to the side room under Mama Scott's house, another hiding place for the kids and for Daddy Scott's homemade moonshine. Larry, Judy and Jean were playing there. Larry had an ice pick and was punching a hole in Bruton snuff cans to make play telephones. Jean had a play phone to her ear, pretending to call the police to her daddy. The Lerner kids often played in this spot, a safe haven for them.

There were all sorts of animals at the Scott's house. Judy's favorite was the peacocks that stayed on the other side of the road, away from Scott's Grocery. Larry's favorite was the horses. When Daddy Scott wasn't drunk, he'd let Larry saddle and ride. Betty Jo's favorite was the hogs, especially the little runt. She loved walking with her granddad to the pigpen late every evening to mix the pig slop, and enjoyed tasting it after it was mixed, although she was warned of the hairy consequences by her granddaddy.

Jean's favorite pet was Barky, the family dog. He'd hold the jump rope in his mouth for her and Betty Jo to take turns jumping.

Emma wondered if Aaron might come and force her to go home. Days passed but there were no sightings of him. The talk around the Scott house was "maybe when he sobered up that Mama Lerner and Daddy Lerner had sent him off for good", but everyone knew that didn't happen.

Meanwhile Emma and the kids helped her parents around the store and in the home. Judy and Larry had the heaviest load and were the big helpers around the Scott's house. Betty Jo had a heart murmur and was a skinny sickly child so was chosen to run the errands with the grandparents.

Daddy Scott with his receding hairline and strawberry nose was hardly ever on his feet long enough to run errands. His moonshine kept him slouched over an old tan English chair most of the time, deep scars from holding the cigarettes too long.

It was a beautiful morning, too early for Betty Jo's inquisitive brown eyes to open. A loud voice kept saying, "Betty Jo, get up! Get up, girl. Get out of that bed. We got to make them runs in Heard County!" Daddy Scott repeated over and over.

Betty Jo scowled. Her least favorite errand was the moonshine run in Heard County with Daddy Scott.

There were so many liquor runs, but she really didn't like that one.

Chicken feathers were flying everywhere. Looked like snow in the house. Daddy Scott, standing over Betty Jo with a belt in one hand and the flat of his other hand beating the pillow, threatening, "Girl, if you don't get outta bed, you're gonna be sorry. Your Grandma wants us to run them errands, and I got to get up to Mahaley's place before her customers get there. Now, c'mon!"

Daddy Scott's fixation with Mahaley Lancaster was getting on Betty Jo's nerves. Mahaley was a psychic from Heard County, Georgia. For all customers, Mahaley charged a dollar for herself, and a dime for her dog, but Daddy Scott didn't seem to mind. He'd walk into the old shack with a handful of change, and waited for their fortunes to be told. She was tall, but stooped, with an apron and eye patch. Sometimes she wore a purple turban, like the gypsies they'd seen. But her favorite was an old Army cap, turned sideways. Going to Mahaley's house always made Betty Jo feel crazy; she felt like something inside her would jump out and get her.

Betty Jo coughed then sneezed. Yawning, she said, "Okay, I'm getting up, these old feathers in my pillow stuck me all night!"

Her feet were slow to touch those old splintered floors. She crawled to the side of the bed, pulled on her little floral flannel gown, sat there looking outside through each little airy crack in the bedroom wall. It would get dark - the sun would shine through the cracks - then it would turn dark again. She hated getting up early, and she was dreading the trip to Mahaley's house. Dr Turner had made a house call just yesterday, and had given her medicine for strep throat that made her sleepy – so sleepy. Her yawns kept coming. She put her hand over her mouth. Sneezing again and again she said nasally, "I'm allergic to these feathers. That's what's making me sneeze a lot, Daddy Scott!" Betty Jo reached down and pulled her gown to her nose and swiped across her face. She sniffed and sniffed.

"I'm not telling you again, little lady." Daddy Scott's voice was echoing through the house.

"Oh, please, Daddy Scott, let somebody else go with you this time! I went last time!"

Daddy Scott's voice was getting louder and louder. "Let's go, girl. I've got you a biscuit and red link from the kitchen, now come on."

"Ouch!" screamed Betty Jo, as she walked across that cold bedroom floor. She started hopping on one foot. "Hold on, Daddy Scott, let me get this splinter out of my foot." He shrugged his shoulders and raised his eyebrows toward her. She'd seen that look before; it put a little pep in her steps then.

Betty Jo slipped on her new Buster Brown shoes, threw on one of her beautiful floral flour sack skirts Mama Scott had stitched for her, grabbed the nearest sweater, then took Daddy Scott's hand and walked with him to the new 1954 Chevy Pickup truck. Betty Jo glanced at the overloaded truck, neatly tied down with a black tarp.

"What's back there?" she asked. Daddy Scott opened the door for her and placed breakfast in her lap. "Nothing, now eat."

"Yes, sir." Betty Jo said quietly as she looked out across the Salem Road to where her brother and sisters were working. Mama Scott had already stirred her siblings and had let Betty Jo sleep in because of fever the night before. Larry was in the woods picking up kindling. His dark, wavy hair covered the black eyes in his tan face. He had on a plaid flannel jacket, tan khakis and brown boots. Judy, tall with dark, curly hair, was overdressed – brown wool coat, and two colorful scarves wrapped her neck. She was stacking the kindling in Jean's arms. Jean, dark curly hair with a cowlick on her forehead, was in contrast underdressed, with rosy cheeks and bare head.

Betty Jo was still complaining to Daddy Scott. "I hate going to Mahaley's house and I hate Heard County," she said over and over again. "Why couldn't I stay with Mama Scott and pick up sticks?"

"Just because! Now sit still and cover up."

Betty Jo's big brown eyes followed the family as she and her granddad pulled onto the Salem Road. Her countenance was very sad but she waved at them. They all gave her a wave and hollered "bye."

Betty Jo and her granddad crossed over Flat Shoals

Creek Bridge and up Fox Hill heading north. There wasn't that much traffic on the road, just a few logging trucks. They rode and rode. Daddy Scott had Betty Jo rolling cigarettes from the Prince Albert can. She reached under his smelly tan jacket to get the tobacco, and pulled out a canteen.

"No, put that back!" he said. "That's my hot coffee yer' Grandma fixed for me." Betty Jo thought she had never smelt coffee that smelt like moonshine before.

It was a windy day. The sun had come out and there were wide swatches of blue sky in between the clouds. Betty Jo's mouth was pressed against the truck window. Cutest little circles formed, along with a smear of green snot.

"Betty Jo, you're making a mess over there," Daddy Scott squawked.

"Sorry," she whispered, as she wiped her nose on her sleeve. There was smoke up ahead. Betty Jo kept her head pressed to the window, and as they passed by a clearing in the field, she looked out and saw dozens of people dressed with white pointed hats and long white robes burning something near someone's home. This scene sent chills up her spine. She began to twist her little body, both hands on the window, and as she stretched to see what those people dressed up like ghosts were doing, a long, green marking went across the window.

"Sit down, Betty Jo," Daddy Scott hollered.

He turned left past an old graveyard to get to Mahaley's little business. It was a long driveway, and a rough ride. After they passed the graveyard, Betty Jo looked out the stained window and saw an old man carrying a flail. The way he was swinging it back and forth made her eyes nearly pop out. She was scared to death. Her thoughts of the ghosts she'd seen down the road now were blotted out with new surroundings.

Daddy Scott's new Chevy had hit every mud hole in that long, winding road. It was an eerie scene, that man with the flail. Daddy Scott tucked his pistol under the seat and kept driving. They heard gypsy flamenco through the woods. Sounded like a party or something. Daddy Scott pulled over, just about landing in the ditch. Someone was coming down the road. As the car met them, Daddy Scott told Betty Jo that the man in the car was one of Mahaley's customers, a well-known lawyer in town.

They pulled up in her dirt yard, the only grass being in little patches around the house. Mahaley cracked the door open, and saw it was Con, and his granddaughter, Betty Jo. Then she opened the door wide. Con nonchalantly got out of the truck, and Betty Jo slid over to get out on her granddad's side. Mahaley had a smile every time she saw him. He was a good customer of hers, and she his. They exchanged their usual greetings and then got down to business. He started unloading the twenty gallons of whiskey he'd put in the back of the truck that morning.

"Hey Con, did you bring my package?" she asked breathlessly. "Gonna give me a discount?"

"Now you know I can't do that - you got more money than anybody in this county!" quipped Con.

" Ah, C'mon now, I'll give you a free reading," she said.

"You know I don't believe in that old witchcraft, Mahaley. But you can read me if you want to," Con joked.

Betty Jo was hoping that they'd make the delivery and fly the coop, but that didn't happen. She walked in behind Daddy Scott, pulling on his drooping khaki pants. Both sat down at Mahaley's kitchen table.

As Mahaley took Betty Jo's hand and traced the lines of her palm, her heart rate increased and her breaths were rapid and shallow. There was a woman lying on a cot in a dark corner who Mahaley had been working on. The woman would draw herself up, look toward Con and Betty Jo, and laugh, a gurgling cackle, before mumbling and collapsing back on the cot.

Mahaley told Con that he would die young, from his own moonshine. He mumbled something to her with his foul mouth.

Betty Jo leaned over, trying to get close enough to hear, and whispered to Daddy Scott, "what did she say was going to happen to you?"

"Aw, nothing! That witch don't know what she's talking about." quipped Daddy Scott.

Mahaley looked at Betty Jo, her mouth twisted to the left, began to snoop. She asked, "How old are you, Betty Jo?"

Her face started to burn, and answered softly, "Close to seven years old."

Then she said, "Well, guess what, Betty Jo. You're going to be a movie star."

Betty Jo started to shake. She really didn't want to be around that psychic, but was sort of tickled that she was going to become a movie star. Her eyes lit up brown fire. She squeezed out a "thank you" with a little smile.

Con told Mahaley to have a good day, and he and Betty Jo got in the truck to finish their errands. Everything had settled down outside. Gypsies had scattered. The man with the flail was nowhere in sight. Even the hooded people were gone.

It was a cold ride back home. Betty Jo could hardly

see out her side of the window. They'd finished all the errands, even picked up a keg of salted fish from Stewart's Wholesale and twenty-five pounds of sausage from Duffey's Meat Packaging place. Daddy Scott's canteen was empty.

Betty Jo leaned over in the seat as they pulled into the store yard. Her heart started to beat fast at what she saw. Her Daddy, Aaron, was there. Betty Jo's mother and siblings were already in the car waiting for her to come home. Emma had given in again; she just couldn't say no. None of them had a happy face.

Betty Jo sat in the car for a minute. "Do I have to go?" she asked, turning to Daddy Scott.

Con's face was sad as he looked at her. "It looks like your Mama has made a decision," he said. "And there ain't nobody in this town who can change her mind once she's said yes to Aaron Lerner. We all learned that a long time ago."

Betty Jo sighed and made her way over to the other car. Her daddy grinned and chucked her under the chin. "You missed me, huh?"

She didn't say anything, just got in the back with the others.

Emma turned and looked at them. "Cheer up. It's gonna be different this time," she said. "Your daddy's promised. He says he's changed."

But the kids knew that nothing had changed. And nothing ever would. It was another long trip up the road back to the little torture house next to the Rock Store.

Chapter Thirteen

As the years passed, turmoil in the Lerner home grew and grew. The Sheriff grew to be a familiar face, and Aaron was taken to the county jail more times than anyone could count. His driver's license was taken away because of all his arrests for DUI. When he was caught driving and the arresting officer asked him his name, he would always laugh and say, "It's big A, little a, r, o, n, I'm telling you once, not telling you again!"

Emma had no doubts that Aaron had been unfaithful to her many times during their marriage. Why should she be surprised? He'd been unfaithful before they were married too. Still, it was a constant grief to her heart.

Aaron even openly flirted with attractive teenage girls in the community. One day a sixteen-year-old girl went missing. Her next-door neighbor called the Sheriff's Department and said that she had run away. The girl had no close relative and no one else took any interest in her whereabouts.

"We had a call last week of a teenage girl running off. She'd gone off with a man of her own free will, so the inquiry was dropped." replied the deputy.

"I don't believe it was this girl. She's very backwards, and sorta keeps to herself."

"All right then, we'll get on it right away." replied the deputy.

Everyone in the community searched their land, corn sheds, barns—everywhere.

Out of the blue one afternoon Aaron said to Emma, "Hey, get in the car—I think I know where that girl might be."

He told Emma to drive to an old abandoned house on Whitesville Road. When they pulled up, it was silent and dark inside, in spite of the sunshine outside.

"Come on, maybe she's in here," Aaron said, and Emma followed him into the house.

They walked through the living room full of trash

and went into a back bedroom. And there she was, hiding behind an old mattress leaning sideways on the wall. She had been crying, and she looked very, very scared.

Aaron held out a hand to her. "Come on, sweetheart," he said, "let's take you back home."

Emma saw the look that passed between them. She didn't say anything, but deep down in her heart she was sure Aaron had actually taken her there, and this shocked her. She wondered yet again what monster she'd married.

Aaron's drunkenness and violent temper continued to cause trouble at home and in the community. One day the sheriff stopped by the house while Aaron was out.

"Ms. Emma, Ms. Bessie, you've got to do something with Aaron."

"We don't know what to do with him. What can we do with him?" Bessie asked, wringing her hands. The days when she'd denied her son was bad had long gone.

"Put him in Milledgeville."

Both women sank into kitchen chairs at this suggestion. Milledgeville was the state asylum for the insane.

Emma and Bessie looked at each other. What else could they do? Emma had done everything that she could for Aaron, but he never did anything to help himself. Both women nodded at the sheriff.

"I don't know what else to do," Emma said. "But I don't know what'll happen to us if he ever gets out."

When Aaron came home, he found the sheriff there to take him to Milledgeville. As the sheriff handcuffed him and loaded him into the car, Aaron screamed at both women, "I'll kill you when I get out. I swear it, I'll kill the both of you."

Aaron spent thirty days in the sanitarium. Emma and Bessie went to see him only once during that period. It was a very upsetting experience. Aaron's knuckles were black and blue from hitting the walls.

"You'd better get me out of this place, Mama." he screamed. Then, looking at the women with pure hate, he added, "You're going to be sorry when I get out!"

Unable to bear the thought of Aaron suffering like this, Bessie arranged for his release, against everyone's advice. Thinking perhaps there would be safety in numbers, Bessie, Emma, Judy, and Betty Jo drove to Milledgeville to pick him up. As soon as Aaron got in the car, wham, his fist hit his mother in the face, and then, wham. Emma received the same abuse.

Soon after this incident, Emma decided to leave him again. She and the children made plans to move back in with her parents.

Chapter Fourteen

Emma and her children caught a ride with her brother, Erbin. He worked at the cotton mill and had gotten off just to take them to the Scott's house. As soon as they pulled in the store yard, Larry saw Daddy Scott across the road in one of his favorite spots. Many Indian graves were located on the property in front of the store. Larry was the brave one. He would throw the rocks off that marked the graves and dig and dig deep down to see if there were really treasures buried with the ancient chiefs. The girls were too afraid, but they would stand and watch him dig. Sometimes they'd slide down muscadine vines in those woods, while Larry would dig for treasures. Barky the little dog was always close by. Judy was superstitious like her grandmother; she didn't want the Indian spirits to come out.

"Hey Buck, go get my shotgun out of the gun case." shouted Daddy Scott.

"Oh, boy," Larry ran as fast as he could. He knew what they were going to do.

Daddy Scott lined up matches on top of the graves, and he and Larry would take turns to see if the red tips would ignite. Larry amused himself with the gun and match game.

"Betty Jo, where are you?" Mama Scott was shouting across the road. "Have ya'll seen Betty Jo?"

"Not in the past two hours," answered Daddy Scott. "Come on, Buck, let's go help yor' Grandma find Betty Jo."

The search started at the pigpen, behind the counters in the store and on an old cot next to the cola box, where she stayed a lot due to sickness. Then they searched the chicken pen, and then the side room where the moonshine was stored. They screamed her name several times. Then Daddy Scott decided to walk down toward the garden. There she was, sitting hidden in the corn patch, playing with the wild gourds and sunflowers. Daddy Scott rattled the tall corn stalks, and she had the most frightening look on her face. She had found another safe place, she thought, away from her Daddy. Only a few days earlier Aaron had turned up and, clutching an almost empty bottle of moonshine in his hand, stumbled around the Scott property, hollering for Emma and the kids to show their faces.

Weeks passed by. The Scotts grew tired of Aaron coming down and disturbing the whole family. Daddy Scott told Emma he thought it best if she moved in with Erbin and his family for a bit. Emma agreed. Another move. The Lerner kids were shipped out again. This time it was Talley Road, about three miles from the Scott house and about a mile from Rock Store.

All the kids enjoyed playing with their cousin, Dianne, a cute blond-haired five-year old girl while her beautiful and chubby little blue-eyed sister, Carrol stayed curled up in her little bassinet. They spent a lot of their time playing up the road at the Shepard house. The Shepards had seven children, four boys and three girls. The oldest Shepard boy told Dianne and the Lerner kids that Talley Road was haunted. He liked to share ghost stories, especially with the girls. He knew it frightened Betty Jo and Jean, and it tickled him to see their eyes enlarge when he was telling his tales.

The younger Shepard boy ate Vick's Salve and picked wild onions, which he'd just bite into. His breath always smelt like something dead. But the kids had to go somewhere, and for the most part, they enjoyed it. They played hard, but like clockwork, they made sure they got home before the sun went down. Being so scared, they'd walk backwards down the dirt road to Dianne's house, making sure that they'd see whatever crept upon them.

When it was daylight, the girls would stop and pick up purple maypops that grew along the roadside to cut into little Mexican dolls. Jean and Dianne would carry the little flower dolls everywhere they went.

One day walking home from the Shepard house, after trying one of those wild onions from the younger Shepard boy, they made their way home on the dirt path through the woods. The Lerner kids and all their first cousins, Dilly, Timmy, Scott, Gayle and Dianne were all holding hands and telling spooky stories and just as they walked past a persimmon tree, everyone started screaming. A large black wild-looking dog was drinking water from the well. Pricking up his ears, the beast looked up—water dripping from its open mouth. They dropped hands, terrified, and took off running to the house. None of them stopped screaming until they reached the porch. The Lerner kids talked about that night for years.

There were no more fun trips to the Shepard house when the inevitable happened. Emma and the Lerner kids moved back in with Aaron. He'd begged and pleaded and promised Emma everything, if she'd only come back. And so she did.

Sadly, Aaron's words came to nothing and the cycle of abuse was repeated. Over and over again, Emma and the children suffered at the hands of their husband and daddy.

Chapter Fifteen

Life went on as usual in the old Rock Store. The traffic on Salem Road roared past, the tingling of the bell around the cow's neck out back, yard man sweeping next to the store, dogs running round chasing the cat, uniformed men getting out of delivery trucks, but still in these quiet surroundings there was bitterness and loneliness in the air.

Emma was tired of living in a domestic crisis. She felt she'd done everything in her power to stay in her marriage. She'd attended counseling with Aaron before they were married. She'd been in several classes over the years. She tried being kind and obedient. That didn't work. Nothing worked.

Emma was sick and tired of her husband's lashing out at everyone who annoyed him. Apart from feeling embarrassed and ashamed that she had chosen a man like that for a husband, he was abusive and was not trying to help himself. All this made Emma feel sorry for Aaron, but what else could she do? Her patience and understanding was just about gone with Aaron's sudden violent temper tantrums. She not only had herself to think of, but four small ones were waiting for her to find help.

Emma, left eye still purple from last week, got up early to go to the store to help Bessie attend to the customers. She was exhausted after another night's struggle with Aaron. She walked out of the little bungalow, leaving all the children asleep. Aaron had passed out at the bottom of their bed.

She looked all around her thinking of her neighbors and friends, with their own particular problems and small happinesses, but none of them like hers. Hers were big, and had followed her for years. She felt her shadow fading. I feel so empty, she thought.

She walked into the store with her droopy face, a half moon smile greeting the customers.

"Hey, Ms. Emma." said one of the colored men as he passed her coming into the store.

"Hey, Ole John. How are you doing today?"

"Oh, just fine, gotta hurry and cut some those big hardwood logs, Ms. Emma. Gotta feed those chiluns' tonight." Ole John smiling, showing his big white teeth as he rushed out, letting the door close easy behind him, going to his old logging truck parked right next to the front of the store. If it had been a little closer, it would've clipped some rocks.

Emma laughed. "You take care, Ole John. Be careful."

"Yes ma'am, I sho' will."

Ole John was a very kind man. He lived way out in the country and was faithful to his family, a great provider, and a wonderful customer. He and his wife had eight hungry mouths to feed.

Emma walked past the hoop cheese to where Bessie was working. "Mum, how do you feel today?" she asked.

"Oh, I was up all night with Harvey. His pains were in his chest and left arm, but he refused to go to the doctor."

"I'm sorry," said Emma. " If I can help you, just let me know."

"I will, honey, but you got your hands full with those children. How about you and Aaron? I see your eye is not getting any better. Are ya'll working your problems out?"

"That's what I want to talk to you about. My eye hurts, my whole body hurts. Judy has scars trying to heal, Jean has bruises, and Betty Jo's jaw hurts constantly. I don't know what I'm gonna do, Mum," said Emma.

"Emma, if you just wouldn't make Aaron angry all the time, he probably wouldn't hit you."

Emma stared at Bessie. "Mum, you know we don't have to make Aaron mad—he's always angry, always abusive to all of us—not just me and the kids, you have scars all over too. I really don't appreciate you thinking that it's my fault. Aaron has acted out since I've known him."

"Well, why did you marry him? It's been nearly twelve years ya'll been together," said Bessie.

"I wish I knew! Everything in me told me not to marry him. But I loved him. Love must be blind. He is so possessive; he pushed and pushed. It's like he backed me into a corral, and wouldn't let me out. I think I married because I was afraid not to, and what would happen if I didn't. You know yourself nobody says "No" to Aaron. And if you do, you pay the consequences. We've been down this road so many times before and I'm tired of it: we all are."

"Well, just try to be kind around him, put more into the marriage and see if it'll work," Bessie said with firmness in her voice, busying herself with stacking sardine cans.

Emma had teary eyes and looked away. She saw that she wasn't getting anywhere with Bessie, who still refused to see the evil man that her son had become, even though she too suffered at his hands.

She sounded like a broken record, just like her marriage. She wanted her problems solved. Should she keep working the hard, exhausting life in the store while her husband lays up drunk, or out causing trouble? Or should she swallow her pride and let Aaron's parents keep supporting her and the children, so she can stay at home? She needed an answer. She felt like she'd get that answer today.

Veronica walked in. She'd been a good listener to Emma and tried to help her all these years but to no avail. She had on a striped apron that made her look like a prisoner when she walked in. Her face flushed from the heat of the kitchen, but looked very beautiful.

"Hey Emma. Hey Mum. How are ya'll today?" Veronica kept talking before they could give an answer. "It's beautiful outside. I brought ya'll some hot cheese and sausage biscuits."

"We're okay, I guess." said Bessie.

Emma was still thinking about what Bessie said: if I'd try to be a little kinder to her son, he might do better. Hogwash. She just smiled, her eyebrows turned upward, biting on her bottom lip, nodded her head toward Veronica, as she reached for her biscuit and took a bite with a sip of RC Cola.

"These are good. I love your biscuits. They taste so much like Mama's. I miss her biscuits, and I miss her," said Emma.

"Well, thank you, Emma. I'm glad you are enjoying them."

"Thanks, Veronica, very good," Bessie said as she turned to go wait on a customer.

Veronica and Emma walked to the back of the store to have some privacy. "Emma, I saw you at the gate yesterday, but it was raining, and before I could find my umbrella to let you in, you were gone. I got busy on the farm. I meant to call you, to see what you wanted," said Veronica.

"I just don't know how much more I can take this, Veronica," Emma blurted out. "I've talked to you so many times; I've talked to Mum and the whole community about my problems but no one is able to help. Aaron's hostility is worse. He's drinking more and more moonshine. He stays out a lot. He refuses to let me speak to my parents. He hurts the children. What can I do? I've got to have help."

Emma was desperate. She knew she sounded like she was begging. What in the world am I thinking? I am begging!

"I don't know, Emma," Veronica said gently. "I've tried to help. Thomas tried too and it seemed to make things worse. You know Aaron is jealous of Thomas. He says Mum and Dad give him everything, and not him. I told you before, I think he's crazy and beyond help. He has no logic. He's lazy, spoiled and everyone gives in to him. His own parents never could control him. I just don't know what to tell you."

Emma had heard this over and over again, not just from Veronica but everyone she has talked to. Agitated, she spilled her drink on the counter. "Oh, get a cloth, quick. My sleeve is wet and sticky."

Veronica went swiftly to the side of the store to an old basin, and brought a couple cold rags back. She handed Emma one; she took the other one and began to wipe down the counter and the splintered floor. She straightened up and pushed some of Emma's hair off her forehead. She reached over and gave Emma a hug. "Look, honey you know I love you, and I'm sorry you've been tormented like you have."

"I know. I love you, too. I chose this life for me; you didn't. It's not your fault. You've been a lot of help over the years."

"I'm just glad I married the brother, and not him," Veronica said, laying a hand on her shoulder. " We've got to get the church members to pray harder for you. I really believe you'll get an answer soon."

"I sure hope so." Emma suddenly felt embarrassed that she'd brought the same old problem up to Veronica and Bessie. But what else could she do? She walked outside to lean up against an oak tree next to the chimps' cage to have a good cry.

Not so long after that, when she was eleven years old, Judy begged Emma to leave Aaron permanently.

"Mother, you've got to listen. Please, please don't be like Mama Lerner. Don't make excuses for Daddy.

He's going to kill us if you don't get help!"

Larry and Betty Jo were standing with her in the kitchen with their eyes bulging out. They'd never heard her talk so forcefully about Daddy before.

Emma said, "You're right, Judy. We've all suffered enough. When he passes out tonight, we'll all go to Herbert's house and see if he will take us to my Daddy's one more time."

Herbert was Aaron's first cousin. He lived three blocks from Rock Store. He worked for CSX Railroad with Thomas; he'd also worked with Aaron a couple of weeks before Aaron came in drunk and was fired. Herbert was a family man and did not condone Aaron's lifestyle.

Sure enough, later that night Aaron got drunk and passed out. Emma called all the Lerner children to the kitchen. "I want ya'll to get your shoes only. We're going to Mama Scott and Daddy Scott's house. We're leaving your Daddy."

Jean, suffering from earache began to whimper,

holding her right ear.

"Shhh, Jean. You're going to wake Daddy up." Judy said, as she dried her face with her Daddy 's handkerchief.

With heavy sobs, Betty Jo pressed the words out, "I'm scared."

"Why, you don't have anything to be scared about. You'll get to see Mama Scott and their pet monkeys."

"I want to see them, but I'm afraid Daddy will come and take us back like he did the other day." Betty Jo's enormous brown eyes looked at Judy so closely she almost started crying.

"I promise you he won't this time," said Judy.

"But you and mother said that the last time, and the time before." said Betty Jo.

Judy interrupted. "We've got to go before he wakes up. Now come on."

Not knowing what to say or do, Larry looked at Judy and followed her. Emma glanced over her shoulder again at Aaron curled up in his drunken stupor and reached down for Jean's rag doll. She picked up Jean and held her close. Judy got Betty Jo and Larry by the hand. All the Lerner kids fled with their mother out the front door. They crossed over the stream, Larry kicking at the rocks and sticks, Jean crying and holding her ear, and Betty Jo trying to figure everything out in her little head. They stepped over large mounds of cow pie, went into the road, and walked to Herbert's house. It was late, and their arrival woke the whole house.

Coming to the door in his pajamas, Herbert said, "Emma, I'll take y'all if you promise me, I mean promise me, girl, that you will never go back to Aaron again—he is going to kill you, if you don't wake up."

"I promise, Herbert. I've learned my lesson."

Herbert, Emma, and the kids squeezed into his car and drove over to the Scott house. Even at her young age, Betty Jo could tell that their expressions were a mixture of "I'm glad to see y'all" and "Oh me, what are we going to do with all these kids?" Beulah was also a little hesitant because she had Emma's other brother living there.

Emma slept in the extra bedroom, and the kids squeezed up on cots in the back room. Betty Jo snuggled down under the covers and listened to the sound of the rain pounding on the tin roof. She fell asleep, feeling sheltered and safe.

This time it was different. Con, Beulah, and Emma knew Aaron would come by the next day demanding his family back, but when he did they didn't allow him to get close to Emma or the children. Beulah made sure they stayed in the house, which wasn't a problem for Betty Jo. She had strep throat again; Dr. Turner had been out and given a penicillin shot, which made her really sick—she'd broken out in bubbles from head to toe. Wrapped up like a mummy and feeling miserable, this was one time that she didn't want to eavesdrop.

When Aaron drove up, Emma talked to him through the screen door while Beulah and Con sat on the porch. Con had a glass of whiskey in his hand, and Beulah had a gun, all loaded and ready to shoot if the need arose. Aaron had to stand out in the front yard on a tall bank full of running salvia to talk to Emma. He was all slouched over with his left hand in his front pocket. Beulah didn't know if he had a pistol or not. She knew though that she'd had a lot of practice over the years and could shoot as straight as he could.

"Emma, I promise you, if you and the kids will come back, I will change."

"Aaron," she said peering through the screen, "You've said that same thing so many times before. It's over now. We've got to move on. You've got to move on. We just can't take it anymore."

"But, I promise you, I will change. I know I can."

"I'm sorry, Aaron."

He turned his head to the side and begged, "Please, just give me one more chance. I'll get more counseling, I promise."

He pleaded and pleaded, but this time, finally, Emma's answer was no, no, no.

In the weeks that followed Aaron always managed to be around. Emma and the kids never knew when or where he would show up, and the threat of that was frightening.

The kids caught the bus at the Scott house and went to Rosemont School. Sometimes Aaron would be hiding behind a tree near the playground and call to them. One time Betty Jo was terrified when she looked in the mirror on the school bus and saw him sitting all the way in the back seat. Betty Jo, the one who had been the bravest before, was the most frightened one now.

The next school morning Emma had a hard time getting Betty Jo out of bed. "Come on now, honey. You've got to get ready—your bus will be pulling up in about twenty minutes."

"Ahhh," she said stretching her toes and pulling the smelly pillow off her head, picking at chicken feathers from the mattress and thumping them to the floor. "I don't feel too good today, Mother."

"Too bad, young lady. Get up, get ready or I'll get

your granddaddy's leather belt."

"But..." Betty Jo tried to finish her sentence but her mother interrupted as she was making up the other side of the bed with nervous energy.

"No buts, just jump up. You'll get to feeling better after you get up, wash your face and eat a bite of breakfast."

Betty Jo rolled her eyes. She sat on the side of the lopsided mattress, got to her feet with disgust. Her worried eyes were stuck together. She began wiping them with her sleeve, "I really am sick."

Emma leaned down to feel her forehead. "Well, you don't have a fever. If you get worse, just tell Ms. Haggler. She'll let you rest in the office."

Ms. Haggler, first grade teacher with dark curls around her oval face, was a sweet person. Betty Jo loved her. She remembered the box Ms. Haggler let her crawl in to tell her story about the Indians. At *storytime* Betty Jo would pretend it was raining and she'd sit in the little cardboard box telling her story. That was her comfort zone, her little city of refuge in the first grade.

Larry came into the room to get Betty Jo for the bus.

"Hush," she screamed, smacking him on the arm. She was fuming cause she had to get out of bed and get ready for school.

"All right, Betty Jo, when you get home, you're getting a spanking for hitting," Emma said as she listened to the screeching tires of the big yellow bus and pushed the children toward the door.

That evening when the school bell rang, Betty Jo had nervously gotten on the wrong bus that day and it was nearly dark before she arrived at the Scott house. There was obvious fear in the house and her mother only gave a lecture. She began stuttering and said she didn't want to go to school any more. Her brother and sisters were cautious, too—none of them wanted to go back to the way things were before.

But then something happened to make that impossible. Finally the legal system began to work the way it should, and "big A, little a, r, o, n" was banned from Troup County.

The sheriff told him if he ever crossed the Georgia line into the county again, he would be locked up for a long, long time.

Emma and the kids felt for the first time that the tide might be turning their way.

Chapter Sixteen

1955

Aaron fled to Mobile, Alabama. He was a drifter now. He had a mark on him, and could not show his face.

The greyhound bus pulled into Station #229 in Mobile. People got up, snatching their paper bags full of belongings and, leaving their soda bottles and cracker wrappers strewn on the seat and floor, stepped off the bus and began to scatter. They obviously knew where they were going.

Aaron on the other hand, stepped off the bus on the cold ground, all alone for the first night ever, away from his family except for the nights he never made it home after passing out on the dance floor. He moved over to let the others pass, then leaned against the bus, head over so his nose was exposed to the light, but his face still obscured by the darkness. What a new and lonely feeling.

He smelled the air. A strong smell of fish was coming from the ocean. What a change. The air back home was much fresher. He stood there thinking: estranged from the family and county he'd always known, what was he going to do now?

He leaned forward dodging a beer bottle from a passing car. Maybe this was his kind of town. He might just show them what a rough neck from Troup County could do, just how mean they are back home.

He picked up his duffle bag, threw it over his shoulders, kicked at the broken bottle on the ground and walked down River Street. He stopped at a window with a navy blue awning, peering in, taking in a different smell and watching the cooks in their white aprons and fluffy caps flipping hamburgers. He stood there for a few minutes before going in. After flirting with the cocktail waitress, he ordered two hamburgers and a large soda pop. Then on top of that a large chocolate shake.

That night he slept in the corner of the bus station and the next day he landed a job, when he had hardly any experience in any job, on a shrimp boat. Captain John's boat went out at 7am and returned to dock around 6pm five days a week.

Aaron made enough money the first day to pitch a drunk that night, but on the next day he jumped on a Greyhound bus that took him to a little town in Alabama bordering Troup County.

As soon as he got off the bus, he reached in his khaki pants for a dime. He found a pay phone and called his mother, Bessie. "Mama, I'm in Lanett. You and Ms. Strickland, that sweet little old lady next door, come and get me."

"Aaron, what in the world are you thinking, son? You've only been gone a couple of days! You know what the sheriff told you. Don't ever come to Troup County again! What if you get caught?" asked Bessie.

Ms. Strickland, her everyday crocheting partner, sat in her dingy wicker rocking chair shaking her head in disbelief. Whispering under her breath, she was saying, Bessie, you should've spanked that child when he was little.

"I'll tell you how to get here. Come on, now." Aaron said with an angry urgency in his voice.

Bessie had felt some relief for those couple days he'd been gone; she couldn't deny it. She was shocked though that he didn't take the sheriff seriously. But he was her son, and she loved him. There weren't no sheriff that could come between a woman her son, was there?

"Come on, Ms. Strickland," she said. "Gather up your crochet. You and me's takin' a ride."

Bessie and Ms. Strickland grabbed their purse and snuff cans. Bessie reached down to get the largest, variegated afghan she and her neighbor had crocheted; she needed something big to hide Aaron.

As the months turned to years, there were many, many trips like this; sometimes he got in the trunk of the car, sometimes in the backseat floorboard. Not many people ever knew about it. Aaron came home, his mother took care of him, the Sheriff would pay a visit, and Aaron would be gone again by daybreak. Each time, the Sheriff told him that if he found him in Troup

County again, there'd be trouble.

Meanwhile, Emma and the Lerner kids moved to a place on a dirt road just off Hamilton Road. A large white house with red shutters was located on the southern side of the road, while four rental houses belonging to Mr. Evans lined up the other side. Across the road was a little church, Oakside Baptist.

It was hard for the family. Emma would not go to the welfare office; she was afraid they would take her children away. She depended on her brothers and parents to drop food by. One of Larry's favorite days was when Daddy Scott brought sugar canes.

As time passed, Emma landed a part-time job at Holmes Drug Store. She also started dating men from Fort Benning, 40 miles away. She met a real nice soldier, Reine Brummer, hometown in Connecticut. Reine Brummer, medium complexion, had short, reddish hair that surrounded his pleasant oval face. He had on a dark green shirt and black pants when he asked Emma to marry him. He was really sweet to all the kids, which they soaked up. He'd play catch with

Larry in the yard, tossing the ball for hours and laughing his mellow laugh. Other times he'd take them all for ice cream, and bought them whatever they wanted from the malt store.

After Aaron and Emma's divorce, Erbin, who had moved to the rental house next to her, went with his sister and Reine Brummer to West Point to get married. Everything was going good - Emma was delighted when she found out that she was expecting. All the little kids were elated.

"Reine, you're so sweet," said Betty Jo, as she and Jean held onto him tightly around his ankles. He smiled. Judy and Larry were as happy as little pigs in slop.

But in a few weeks Reine Brummer was picked up by several military police. One of the officers told Emma that Reine Brummer was married to a lady in Connecticut. They walked him to a jeep and took him to the brig located in Fort Benning.

The Lerner kids were very disappointed. They thought their mother had found a good Daddy for them. Emma was broken-hearted. Reine Brummer had been perfect - so different from Aaron. Gentle, big-hearted, full of laughter. Why did he have to be married, too?

Emma developed toxemia during her pregnancy, and Jackie, a beautiful 4 lb. baby girl with fuzzy hair and big brown eyes, was born. For a while, Emma was busy with the kids, bringing up Jackie and seeing that the others all went to school.

When Jackie was a toddler, Emma started dating a man that drove a cab. Charles had red hair, freckles and was poorly dressed when he was brought home to meet the Lerner kids. Emma seemed to think he was great - another Reine Brummer perhaps. But the kids knew better. They just had to take one look at Charlie to know what sort of man he was. He was just like their daddy.

On the day Emma and Charles was married, he whipped Jean with a peach limb because she asked to see his chigger bites. He could see the hate in the Lerner kids for him. They could not understand why their mother would marry a man with similarities as their real Daddy. They'd talk about some nights after dark, when they'd had enough of listening to their mom sob herself to sleep in the bedroom down the hall.

"She doesn't think she deserves any better," was Larry's theory. "She thinks that's all she can get."

"Maybe any man is better than no man," Judy Ann said.

On a trip to Charles' parents house in Alabama, he made all the children sit in the back seat with him, so he could have control. He knew Jackie was not his child, and he would push the baby bottle into her little impetigo-infected mouth. She would cry and try to get out of his lap, but he would push harder. The Lerner kids wanted to help their little sister, but they were helpless, and so was Emma.

There came a time when Emma would come home from her part-time job and her husband was not there with the children. Apparently, he had grown tired of all the little footsteps around the cold, cold house and he moved back to Alabama with his parents, and was never seen by Emma and her children again. This called for a celebration. The Lerner children held hands and went round and round, singing happy songs, jumping up and down. Emma couldn't help but feel relieved too.

Even with Emma's part-time job, the Lerner kids' stomachs still growled loudly. Larry would get on his bike sometimes and ride for miles to his cousin's house to eat with him. Betty Jo loved watching Jackie. She would place her on her hip and go next door, to the black family whose sons picked cotton with them on Mr. Evan's farm. Betty Jo would take milk, chocolate or whatever she could find to their little boy Clarence, and trade it to the black family for dried butterbeans, or collard greens.

She'd walk in the little house, one built just like theirs, and sit at their table. She would feed her little sister, then go outside and play with the little colored kids.

Larry, Betty Jo and Jean were at the house alone one day, hungry again. It was real quiet next door at their aunt and uncle's. They weren't at home; both worked first shift in the cotton mill. Larry and Betty Jo scrambled around in the kitchen and found some pinto beans. There was no electricity in the house, so the Lerner kids decided to cook outside. Larry couldn't find the long-stem Domino matches, so he and Betty Jo rubbed a metal and rock together to get a spark under the old black washtub in the backyard. Even after Larry had removed the scrubbing board and washed the old pot, a smell of lye soap was still present.

Larry heard a noise out front. Another truck had pulled in - a familiar sound around their house. One day it was the utility man to turn off the electricity, but today the Skinner man had come to get the kitchen rug. The Skinner man knew the family, hated his job, so he tore the rug up instead of taking it back to his workplace.

After watching the furniture man do his job, Larry and his siblings went back to the cooking pot. It took a while to cook those beans, but they touched the spot in their bellies.

The Lerner kids had good days and bad days on Evans Drive.

Chapter Seventeen

Winter 1958

All the Lerner kids were wrapped up with toboggans, coats and several pair of socks. It was cold inside and outside the house, so the children elected outdoors. Her uncle's voice came from far off, "Betty Jo, come quick, you have a call."

She had seen a telephone many times, but hardly ever talked on one. She looked surprised, but ran as fast as she could to her uncle's house.

"Hello."

"Hello," a voice answered on the other end. "This is Santa Claus - I hear you've been a good girl, been taking milk to your little neighbor - what do you want for Christmas, little girl?"

The voice on the other end was Mr. Sharp. He had a children's talk radio show in the daytime. He'd met Emma at the drugstore next to the radio station, and

Emma had asked him to call Betty Jo and pretend to be Santa Claus.

Betty Jo was elated. "I want a pretty baby doll with a bottle, that's all!" she answered shyly.

"Okay, ho-ho-ho." Mr. Sharp ended the call.

Betty Jo felt like a movie star. Everyone around her started laughing, just watching all her expressions. Her aunt hovered over her with a plate of oatmeal cookies. Larry and Jean held out their hands.

Betty Jo's uncle Erbin had given her the nickname of "Juggie." He said, "Juggie, what do you think about that?"

She had stopped shivering as she had come out of the cold into their warm house. She turned around, smiled at her aunt and uncle, and hollered, as she ran back outdoors, "Thank you, Uncle Erb."

She went out thinking, me—a good girl. I can't believe Santa Claus called me.

The single-seated outhouse was about thirty yards

behind Emma's rental house on Evans Drive, and backed onto a cornfield. It could be pretty scary in the dark. Larry hardly ever had anyone watch for him when he went to the toilet at night, but the girls sorta helped each other out, standing in the backyard with a flashlight. During the week, the Lerner kids made sure they had a lot of dried corncobs from the field lined up next to the toilet. Sometimes, if they were lucky, they'd furnish the toilet with the Sears catalog.

One night Larry got off his pallet and just had to go to the toilet.

"Hey, Sis. Will you stand at the back door for me? I gotta go to the toilet real bad?"

All the girls looked at each other, trying to figure out which sister he was talking to. "Is he talking to me?" asked Betty Jo. "I think he's talking to you, Judy."

"No, he knows I'm not going. It's just too cold out there."

All the girls started to agitate him. They got under a white sheet and started making ghoulish sounds.

Larry didn't like this at all; he was holding his stomach in pain, with his legs crossed. He kicked at the sheets, "Somebody walk out there with me now. Hurry."

No one in the house wanted to go with him. It was just too cold outside—clouds covered the moon. Scarecrows with blue overhauls, plaid shirts and straw hats decorated the cornfields. There were all kinds of noises out in the cornfields. When the wind blew, the cornstalks shook and made its music. It was a very familiar sound in the daytime, but very scary at night. After Larry reached the outhouse, Judy and the girls decided to wrap sheets around them and go outside and try to scare him. They went to the linen closet and pulled all the white sheets down from the dusty shelves. Poor bubba, it was hard being the only boy in the family.

Emma was at work, so all the girls, shivering and shaking, slipped out the front door, quietly went around the house to spook their brother. But before they could get close enough to the tilted, beat-up splintered outhouse door, something else had spooked him, and he came running out of the toilet with pants on the ground. Corncobs and sheets from the Sears catalogue were strewn about. The girls hit the ground laughing.

By this time Larry was mad and chased those sisters of his back into the house. "Ya'll are the meanest sisters in the world," he screamed, "couldn't I've had just one brother out of all you sisters? Brats, you're all just brats and I can't stand neither one of you." He was still shaking in his tracks.

Nothing in that little house settled down until their mother walked in from a hard night's work.

All the Lerner kids were speaking to each other the next day. Mamaw Lerner had been by and had left each of them a nice toy in a neatly wrapped box with a Kroger sack of pecans and a large bag of orange jellies, the kids' favorite.

Chapter Eighteen

Many years passed, some of them happy and some of them just-so. The 1960s came and Emma was better without Aaron, and although her kids sometimes went barefoot and hungry there wasn't a shortage of love. One day Emma was watching them all. They were out in the yard, doing chores. So tall, she thought. When did they get so tall?

Betty Jo seemed to sense their mother watching and she looked up and waved at Emma. Emma waved back. My babies are all grown up, she thought in surprise. Where did the years go?

Aaron continued to cross the Georgia line, helped by his mother and Ms. Strickland. He had been caught a couple times crossing over. He spent about six months in the Meriwether Prison Camp. As soon as he was released, he went back to his old tricks.

After a while Aaron began living a hobo life,

jumping trains in Alabama, Florida, Texas, and Georgia. Once, a CSX train was traveling down the tracks in Bessemer, Alabama, and Aaron had a stroke and fell off. Several other hobos were camping out around the tracks. One of them had seen an object come out of the train.

"Hey man, did you see that?" The hobo poking at the campfire nodded.

Two of the hobos ran to the tracks to see what it was. It was Aaron in a fetal position having a seizure. The hobo reached in Aaron's pocket and pulled out a dime to make the emergency call. He also snagged several quarters to put in his old torn plaid jacket. The ambulance arrived in less than five minutes and took Aaron to the nearest hospital in Bessemer.

Thomas, Veronica and Betty Jo went to Bessemer to visit Aaron. He had lost so much weight—down to about 120. He looked so pitiful. Betty Jo felt her fear shrivel away to nothing as she looked down at this pitiful wreck of a man.

She drove him to West Alabama Hospital in Lanett.

On the way, she spotted some pretty, shiny wheat on the side of the road. "Oh, look. I wish I had some of that dried wheat." It was really glistening in the sun; each piece filled with glitter.

"Stop the car. Pull over." Aaron said. Giving no signal she pulled over to the side, in a very congested area. He got out and picked the wheat - and Betty Jo keeps it to this day, all wrapped up in one of her cedar chests. She wanted something pretty to remember him by.

Betty Jo tried to be patient with Aaron. But to this day she asks herself "why"? Why would anyone in her right mind have anything to do with him? One of the meanest men that ever lived! Judy, being the oldest, remembered *too* much, and did not ever want to see him. Larry and Jean wanted to get even. Once, many years later, Larry and Jean found out where he lived—at a boarding house in Prichard, Alabama and traveled there to see him.

On the Greyhound bus for five long hours, they talked and talked about what they were going to say to him when they got there.

"I think I'll just bop him up against the side of his head, knock them big blue eyes out," said Larry.

"I think I'll kick him where it hurts," said Jean.

They laughed uncontrollably. The other passengers turned and gave them a stare.

A yellow cab took them to the address he thought they'd given him, but the man there said he did not know the person they were asking for. The cab turned around and tried another house. It was a big white boarding house, with a screened-in porch covering most of the property. They walked past the monkey grass and flowers lined up along the sidewalk. Rose bushes of all colors were lined up and down a red brick wall. That part of town was nice, nothing like the family thought it would be. Larry, being the oldest, knocked on the door. A nice lady, a little on the stocky side, came to the door. "Can I help you?

"Is Aaron here?" Larry asked, as he turned and smiled at Jean still thinking about their little plot on the bus.

"Yes, he is. May I ask your names?"

"I'm Larry. This is my sister, Jean. I think he'll remember us. We came all the way from LaGrange to see him."

It was like Larry was desperate, that he was begging, and wanted to make sure she didn't turn them away.

"Of course, come in. Your father has spoken a lot of you guys."

That's strange, Larry thought, he hadn't seen them for years - but he'd have to know what they looked like cause they both favored him, even if Larry had brown eyes.

Aaron, dressed in faded Jeans and boots, came to the door like he'd been expecting them. He placed one arm on Larry's shoulder and shook with the other hand. Then he leaned forward to give Jean a hug. She stood there pulling back like she was uncomfortable with him doing that.

Aaron stepped back and held the door for them to enter. The living room was large, with furniture that had been overhauled a few times. A stained gold velvet sofa stretched against one wall, and the window facing them looked out over the placid gray surface of the Mobile bay. But like Jean and Larry's heart, the room felt cold and untouched.

Larry sat down in a single chair and Jean in a glider rocker next to him.

"Did ya'll have a hard time finding the house?" asked Aaron.

"Well, actually we did - the cab driver took us to a house down the street, the one with the bulldog in the front yard, you know the house with the chain fence and the most prettiest flowers in the world. He got confused, said he was dyslexic, and couldn't see too well," said Larry.

Everyone laughed.

"Well, I'm glad you found the right one."

"Yeah, me too," answered Larry, twisting and

turning in an uncomfortable chair. His fanny was numb from the long ride on the Greyhound on a busy interstate. "This is a really nice boarding house. I wondered all these years if you lived in a house, boat or what. But this is really nice. And the yard is so pretty. How long have you lived here?" Larry, nervous, rambled on and on, still squirming in his chair.

"Well, I stayed in motels and commercial boats when I first left LaGrange, actually the first night I slept curled up in a bus station," said Aaron.

You mean when you were banned from Troup County, LaGrange Georgia, Larry thought as he stared his Daddy looking through those big blue eyes.

"Then I bumped into this nice lady in a restaurant, I mean a nice bar." He chuckled as he peered over his shoulder at Ms. Brodin the lady who had greeted them at the door. Her sour look meant that she didn't appreciate him speaking of her in this fashion, even if it were true. That was just something you didn't tell kids you hardly even knew, children that he'd not seen in a long time.

Larry broke his stare and smiled at Jean. She was still smiling; she was waiting for the word attack. She sat in her off-white glider chair, constantly pushing her shoulder bag up thinking my brother is really showing off being nice to this guy that the family hated so much, I'll never forgive or forget what he's done to our family, especially mother. Has my brother forgot our mission?

Aaron put the flat of his hand on Jean's knee. She snatched her left leg to the side letting him know not to touch her.

Aaron didn't seem to notice. "What have you been up to lately, Jean? How have you been doing?

"Okay, I guess." She was short and to the point. What she'd like to talk about is something that she knew he wouldn't like, the past for one thing.

"You know," Aaron said, leaning over to Jean, "I tried to see you guys many times, but after your mama signed those extradition papers, I didn't have a choice. But I really love ya'll and missed you so much." Aaron continued, "and I was hoping that your mama and I could've worked things out, but she up and got married again."

He leaned closer to Jean, close enough that she could see the wrinkles and bags under his blood-shot eyes. She wondered for a moment if he ever slept, like she'd seen him so many times before in his drunken stupor.

"Oh, so you're saying its Mother's fault. I don't think so." Jean was sitting on the edge of her chair about to fall in the floor. "What I remember as a small child, I don't think there was anything else for mother to do but leave you." Jean was getting all riled up. She was ready to make a tackle. She snuck a glance at Larry.

"No, I'm just saying," he went on, his face hot like the noonday sun. "If...

Ms. Brodin broke in. She had a way of seizing the conversation. She pretended not to see the anger in the two children. "Well, we're delighted to have you two. Would you care for a glass of cold tea or coffee? I just made chicken salad sandwiches if you'd care for one."

"No ma'am. Larry answered, crouching forward in his chair. We just ate a pack peanut butter crackers and a double cola on the way over."

They pretended they were glad to see him and accepted an invitation to stay overnight.

Aaron started drinking as soon as the sun went down. He drank beers at first, then went and got a bottle of moonshine from some hiding place. "Don't tell Mrs Brodin," he said with a cackle of laughter. "She'll get all sour, just like your mother used to."

"Our mother had reason to get sour," said Jean.

Larry stood up. "I don't ever remember her being sour," he protested. "She was good to you, and all you did was make her pay. Just like you made us pay."

Aaron swigged his moonshine and stared at them through bloodshot eyes. "Your mother, yo' grandmother, yo' granddaddy and all you kids was a no-good...

Larry lashed out so fast that Aaron never knew what hit him. Larry had learned from an early age how to punch, watching his father had been some kind of masterclass. And Jean was practiced from all those fights Aaron had made her have with her sisters. She stepped in, looking down at him, and her boot flashed out. "I'm gonna whip you," she said, tears streaming down her cheeks. "Just like you whipped us and momma all those years. This is payback."

When they'd had payback, the brother and sister jumped on a Greyhound bus back to LaGrange. Both of them, eyes filled with blue and brown fire, bragged to all the passengers how they'd finally got revenge. "This is the day I've been waiting on," Larry shouted as he hit the back of the seat in front of him like he was playing the drums. Larry later told Betty Jo, "That whippin' made up for everything he done to us."

Betty Jo had different feelings. She loved Mamaw Lerner and stayed in touch with her son, and he wrote her letters.

Chapter Nineteen

In 1974 Thomas called Betty Jo on her job and said that her Daddy had been stabbed eight times on a shrimp boat. He and another employee, both drinking, were fighting. The knife went in his back all the way through. She traveled to Mobile and called her pastor in her church and asked that he and his members pray at the cottage meeting that night.

When Betty Jo reached the hospital, Thomas met her at the door. "Betty Jo, your Daddy died on the operating table, but a miracle happened! The doctors could not believe it. They said Aaron was cursing and screaming at the devil. 'Devil, devil, get away from me, you sorry devil! My feet are burning. Stop, devil, go away!'" Thomas took a deep breath. "Veronica and I just can't believe it," he said.

Betty Jo was admitted to the hospital with migraine headaches. The doctors ran several tests on her. Her main complaint, besides the pain, was having the same dream every night. Her dream was that she could hear a train coming down the tracks. The whistle was always blowing loud. Cinders from the train were covering the trees lined up down the train tracks. She envisioned her dad on a vessel floating out to sea. She and the other Lerner kids were on another boat. She saw her Daddy on his boat, The Lerner. It was always getting close to her and her siblings. This was very frightening. In her dream, she would scream, "Go faster, Larry. Go, go faster—he's catching up with us!"

"This is as fast as it will go, Betty Jo. It won't go any faster." This was always Larry's answer in her dream.

Betty Jo had the same dream for years. She went to many doctors, but nothing helped. As her dad reached her boat in the dream, someone would be calling out to her, "Wake up, Betty Jo, it's only a dream."

Betty Jo continued to write Aaron. He wrote her back. One Saturday she was outside cleaning around her beautiful azaleas. She glanced over her shoulder and saw the mail delivery truck at her box. He ran early on this gorgeous day. She washed up and walked down the graveled driveway to the freshly painted large yellow mailbox. She gathered up magazines and pamphlets and on the bottom of the stack was another letter. The old fear rose in her so quickly, like a hand at her throat, hands shaking as she reached for the letter addressed to her.

She turned and walked past the high neatly trimmed hedges that enclosed the driveway. Hundreds of plump shiny black birds were fluttering about, diving to the ground for leftover breadcrumbs. The pleasant look Betty Jo had all morning now turned sour. She remembered the last letter was okay, but the one before that one was just too cavalier, having to pay his debts so he wouldn't have to go to jail. What is there to worry about?

She walked up twelve long steps hearing each sound like thunder, opened the patio door to the sunroom, threw the magazines and pamphlets down on a shiny oak vanity then walked to her favorite green glider to open the letter. Her stomach was still in a knot. She slit open the coffee stained envelope and took out a letter, ironed out the wrinkles and started reading:

"Dear Betty Jo: Hope you are doing fine. I'm fine, except for the pneumonia that lingers. Call me at 334-555-5555 when you get this letter. I have a favor to ask. Love always, Daddy."

Betty Jo leaned back in her comfortable glider. She tiptoed down that memory chute and found herself revisiting her childhood memories.

She went into a deep sleep then came the recurring dream— the loud whistle on a train and out in the water her dad standing at a smoking lamp on a vessel and the Lerner children on another boat, and she woke up screaming, "Go faster, Larry, go faster, he's catching up with us."

She awoke when a tree limb fell on the roof. Her head resting in her elbow she looked around the room and sighed. She sat there and tried to figure out if these things had really happened in her life, and why did she let her Daddy use her? Why did she feel like she owed him everything?

When she and her family escaped from him a long time ago she shouldn't've communicated with him. She should have listened to Judy. Maybe his craziness passed down to her. "Nonsense," Betty Jo whispered, shaking herself awake, "Get up and go call him."

Agitated at herself she scurried down the narrow hall next to the dining room table, reached over the wainscot wall trimmed with a burgundy and green floral pattern for the phone. She slowly dialed the number in her dad's letter. She ran her fingers over the smooth off-white phone, wiping dust and then rubbing it off on her blue denim skirt. Her heart thudded in her chest. One ring. Two rings, then three rings. Her palms got sweaty then as she was reaching to hang up she heard a female's voice. "Hello."

"Hi, who's speaking, please?" asked Betty Jo.

"I'm the housekeeper at Springfield Motel. Who would you like to speak with?"

" Aaron Lerner. He left this number for me to call," Betty Jo said with her voice shaking.

"Just a minute," said the housekeeper, "let me check with the manager. He's on a quick break."

"Okay, thank you".

The nice lady on the other end told Betty Jo to wait and then she came back on the line. Betty Jo could hear the cleaning lady as she took steps and she could hear her talking in the background. Then the steps got louder, and the lady came on the phone, "Mr. Lerner is in Room 333. Let me connect you."

"Thank you so much."

Betty Jo looked down at the cup of Folgers in her hand, unmoved. I don't know what I'm thinking, why am I calling?

Then a hoarse voice came on the phone. "Hey Betty Jo, I've been waiting on you to call—what took so long?"

Betty Jo's face was the noonday sun at that moment. "I just received your letter today. What's going on?" asked Betty Jo. She reached for her large ceramic mug, took a sip of cold coffee.

"Well, I have some good news," her Daddy said sounding like a schoolboy.

"What is it?" she asked taking in a deep breath and still can't believe she is wasting her time on a phone call. The day is gorgeous and she should be outside in the yard where it is calm and peaceful.

"I want to get married."

"Get married?" Betty Jo asked.

"Yes, there's this nice young lady I met down here in Mobile and she's perfect, the prettiest thing you ever did see."

Betty Jo let out a sigh. "I can't believe it," she said as she leaned over the snack table and grabbed a handful of peanuts.

"Can't believe what?" asked Aaron.

"I just can't believe you're wanting to get married after all these years. Who is she?" asked Betty Jo, crunching on her nuts.

"Her name is Linda. She's from Texas. Her parents

have been visiting kinfolk down here in Mobile for a couple of weeks. I bumped into them out in the motel lobby. They're real nice people and she's twenty-seven years old."

"Twenty-seven?" Betty Jo asked trying hard not to anger him.

"Yep, and she's never been married. She has some kind of handicap - her parents go with her everywhere."

"Handicap?" Betty Jo asked with concern in her voice. "What kind of handicap?"

"Oh, I don't know, she's not crippled or anything like that, but she draws a disability check from Social Security. Hey, Linda's sitting right here. You want to speak to her?" he asked.

"No, I don't want to speak to her. Don't put her on the phone. What happened to Mrs. Brodin?" Betty Jo asked, still very agitated and sweat rings starting to form under her arms.

"What happened to who?" he asked.

"Mrs. Brodin, the lady at the boarding house over in Prichard?" Betty Jo was standing at the picture window with her forehead pressing against it watching a gold and white cat chase the birds from the food strewn on the ground.

"Oh, her? Yeah, her kids don't want her around me anymore. They kicked me out. That's why I'm at Springfield."

"Why did they kick you out?" asked Betty Jo.

"Well, you know Mrs. Brodin liked to spend money on me. She'd keep me in fancy boots and shirts, and she'd take me on vacations to all parts of the world. Guess the kids thought she was wasting too much money on me."

"Oh, I see. Did you say Linda is twenty-seven? Does she know you're nearly fifty years old?" asked Betty Jo.

This question really irritated Aaron. "I don't see why that matters," he snapped. "She even said that I didn't look my age and that I look much younger. Are you going to the courthouse for me? Are you still there? Can you hear me? You haven't even heard what I'm asking you to do, have you?"

A breath of fire seemed to come at Betty Jo from the receiver. She held the phone away from her face. She wanted to scream at him but decided to agree with him. "Yes, I'll go to town first thing in the morning and get those papers for you. Then I'll call you back at this number."

Betty Jo slammed the phone on the wall. Aaron handled her just like he did her mother and grandmother.

Betty Jo tossed and turned all night. She wanted to get her Daddy's arrangements all settled so maybe she could have a little time off before she heard from him again. She got up bright and early to go to the courthouse. Then at lunch she took her fast food meal to her house to get the phone number to call her Daddy. She walked into the house, threw her keys down on the kitchen table next to the sunflower arrangement. Then she reached for the phone.

"Springfield Motel, may I help you?"

"May I speak to Aaron Lerner," asked Betty Jo, spearing an olive from her salad with a fork.

"Just a moment, please," says the voice on the other end of the line.

"Hey, Betty Jo," Aaron said.

"Hey, how are you?"

"Fine, did you get my divorce papers?"

"Yes, I did," Betty Jo said with enthusiasm, "but I'm afraid it's bad news for you."

"What do you mean - bad news?" Aaron asked with concern.

Betty Jo picked up a copy of Aaron and Emma's divorce papers. " It says you have no right to remarry." She walked into the sunroom. Lighthouse sketches hovered on the mint-green walls, and on the mantle just under the candle sconce was a display of sailboats. Betty Jo's love for nautical scenes must've come from her Daddy. "It also says you are thousands behind in child support."

Then Aaron interrupted. "There must be a mistake somewhere. Are you sure?"

"Absolutely," Betty Jo said, but somehow she got the feeling that her Daddy expected more out of her. He was very disappointed.

"Well, thanks anyway. I'll talk to you guys later." He hung up.

A week later on a Wednesday the phone rang. Betty Jo answered and she knew immediately that her Daddy was drunk. He was slurring and angry, and she could hear him kicking the furniture as he told her that Linda's parents had stopped him from seeing her, and if they ever saw him again that they would have him locked up. Then they traveled back to western Texas.

Chapter Twenty

1981

Outside a cold rain had begun to fall. Aaron had attended his ship captain's funeral that morning in Mobile, Alabama. It was a dreary day. He sat on the side of his bed, homesick, wanting to see his mother. The rain spattered on his motel window. He reached for the phone to call his mother's neighbor.

After eight long rings, Ms. Strickland answered the phone. "Aaron, she's not here; she's been in the hospital about a week now. The doctor wants to put in a pacemaker but your mom refused. She's not going to make it, Aaron. Bessie always thought she would pass before spring."

This really saddened Aaron and made him feel lonely. He went to the nearest pub in Mobile, drinking and drinking. His mind went back to all the times his mother, Bessie and Ms. Strickland picked him up at the Greyhound station near the Georgia line, hid him in the trunk or in the backseat with a crocheted afghan. Tears rolled down his cheek. "I wish I'd been more respectful to my mom," he told one bartender. Then he asked for more drinks.

When Aaron got back to the motel, there were several messages for him to call home. He knew. Thomas got clearance for his brother to come to their mother's funeral. She was beautiful in a bronze casket with pink backing. Dogwood trees and white doves were in the background. After the funeral, her body was taken to Shadow Lawn Cemetery.

The family gathered around. Cars and trucks made a faint roar in the distance. The air was sharp and clean with a feeling of spring in it. Daffodils were peeking around the tombstones.

Aaron stood next to Thomas around the casket. Veronica kept her distance from Aaron. She stayed close to Emma, Judy and her immediate family. Aaron looked over the cascading flower wreaths and for the first time in twenty-seven years he got a glimpse of Emma and Judy. With his whole life there in front of him his thoughts were to speak to Emma, but the two women didn't stay to mingle with Aaron, family or friends gathered at the cemetery.

Betty Jo was given Aaron's part of Bessie's insurance money and was to issue as needed. Aaron worried her so much at work and home wanting her to wire his money that when it came down to a few hundred, she closed the account and sent it all to him and marked Paid in Full.

Betty Jo only heard from Aaron a few times after his mother died. She got concerned one day in April 1985 when she hadn't heard from him for a while and started calling nursing homes, hospitals and other businesses in the Mobile area. She called a convalescent home in Prichard, Alabama near Mobile.

A woman answered the phone. "Yes, your daddy is here."

"Can I speak with him?" asked Betty Jo.

"I'm so sorry," the woman replied. "But your daddy is really sick. He had a stroke."

Betty Jo felt the shock run through her. "Is he going to die," she asked softly, wondering whether she really wanted to hear the answer.

"I can't say," the woman said. "Do you want that I give him a message?"

Betty Jo took a deep breath. What message was there? She didn't know what to say for a moment, but then she spoke quickly. "Tell him Betty Jo is on the phone… and ask if I can do anything for him."

The woman was gone for a while, and the minutes ticked by. Betty Jo held the phone to hear, listening, watching the cars go by out on the road. People out there were going about their normal lives, and her daddy had had a stroke. She felt hollow inside.

There was rustling sound and the woman came back on the line. "He says he'd like to have a pack of cigarettes."

Knowing it wasn't good for him, Betty Jo didn't send any.

Aaron Lerner died on July 5th, 1985 in Mobile,

Alabama. Five days later an officer searched his billfold and found Betty Jo's telephone number. The funeral home mortician wanted to know if the family wanted the body; if not, Aaron would be given a pauper's funeral. Thomas asked the mortician, "What was the cause of death?"

"He died from lung lesions that were probably caused from the shrimp boat stabbing years ago."

Most people knowing Aaron's life would say he didn't deserve a decent funeral.

But the Lerner kids got together and discussed what to do and even though they had not been treated right when they were children at home with Aaron, they decided that everyone deserved a decent funeral and after all this was their father. "Whatever he did, he's still family. We can't let him go into a pauper's grave! We should bury him by his mother and father."

Thomas, Larry and Betty Jo had the body transferred to LaGrange. They all gathered at the funeral home.

When Betty Jo saw what her dad had become, it broke her heart. He had long gray hair and a long gray beard. He looked pitiful. Obviously, no one in Mobile had cared anything about him except for the boarding house lady that died years before.

All the Lerner kids attended the funeral at Pleasant Grove near the Rock Store, although they all had mixed emotions. Emma didn't go to the funeral. She'd said goodbye to Aaron years ago, and she said she didn't need to do it all over again.

Aaron Lerner was buried in Shadow Lawn Cemetery next to his mother, Bessie. The Lerner's rebel son had made it home to Troup County.

Epilogue

Emma—lived to be 80 years old and died in 2004. She was active in her church after giving her heart to the LORD in 1976

Judy—still resides in Troup County Ga. and is happily married

Larry—was killed on Elm St. in a tragic construction accident in 1987

Betty Jo—still resides in Troup County

Jean—*died at Emory Hospital in 1985 one month after Aaron*

Jackie—*still resides in Troup County Ga. and* enjoying her grandchildren

Bessie & Beulah —died at age 79

Harvey—died in the fifties

Con—died in the early sixties